Through the Dark Night

RASPBERRY RIDGE
BOOK ELEVEN

JESSIE GUSSMAN

Contents

Acknowledgments

Cover art by Julia Gussman
Editing by Heather Hayden
Narration by Jay Dyess
Author Services by CE Author Assistant

Listen to the unabridged audio for FREE performed by Jay Dyess on the Say with Jay channel on YouTube. Get early access to all of Jay's recordings and listen to Jessie's books before they're available to the general public, plus get daily Bible readings by Jay and bonus scenes by becoming a Say with Jay channel member.

One

Raspberry Ridge 2 miles.

Shannon adjusted her grip on the steering wheel, her hands sweating. Just two miles until she was...home? It felt like she was coming home. But she didn't want to. She left for a reason, and she hadn't looked back, taking her two children and leaving with her husband, heading out of the town she grew up in.

Too many painful memories.

Now, with her marriage blown to bits and her children scattered, leading new lives of their own, she felt like this was the only place for her to go.

Sure, she could have stayed in Detroit, but...who wanted to live in Detroit?

She had friends there, but they were city friends, friends from the suburbs. People she waved to, saw when she was out walking, knew by first name, and that was pretty much it.

They weren't the kind of friends who knew the details of her life, both the good and the bad, the ugly.

Most of the time, that wasn't what she really wanted. But she missed the soul-deep knowledge that small towns had. Sure, there was gossip, and nothing was off-limits, but there was a caring there, a concern, a "you're one of our own, and we will take care of you" kind of attitude that was completely lacking in the generic Detroit suburb.

She swallowed hard and took a breath. Why was she nervous? Why was she scared?

Maybe it wasn't nervousness or fear but more a knowledge that the memories were here, and she'd never faced them. Everyone said time healed, and Shannon believed that to be true. Surely allowing time to put a buffer between her and the sharpness of the pain was a coping mechanism that would someday be acceptable in the eyes of the world.

She wouldn't change the fact that she left.

She might have changed some of the decisions that she made when she was younger, but she pushed that thought aside as well. Her life was what it was, and there wasn't anything she could do to change it now. The decisions had been made, consequences had been lived through, and there was no turning back.

However, sometimes a person got to a fork in the road and they had to make a decision about how they were going to move forward.

She already made that decision too. She decided that she was going to sell the house in the suburbs and move to Raspberry Ridge.

And now, here she was, almost back in her hometown for the first time since she left almost two decades ago, and she felt like turning around and running.

She had no idea where she would run to.

As her white SUV crested the last hill, the expanse and magnificence of Lake Michigan came into view. The sun glittered on the water, and Shannon's breath caught in her throat. Grateful that the road was deserted, she pulled to the side of the road and came to a stop, her hands resting on the wheel, her eyes on the immense and beloved lake in front of her.

This was her last view as she left town all those years ago, her heart cracked and broken, and she wasn't sure she would ever be able to function without pain again.

The pain had faded, although she had come to understand that it would never truly go away. One could not lose one's daughter—a child that had come from one's own body, one that she had nurtured and cared for for the first fourteen years of her life—and not expect there to be a permanent mark on her soul.

She pulled both lips in between her teeth as she looked at the rippling water, the sunlight glistening, always moving, shimmering and shining, then dark, cloudy, and dreamlike.

She couldn't figure out whether it felt good to be home, or maybe she just felt relief. Relief that she had a soft place to land after all this time.

Of course, the landing might not be as soft as what she hoped. She shoved that thought aside. She would face that when she had to, but first, she had to get into town.

Taking one last long look at the shimmering lake in front of her, she took another deep breath, as though to fortify herself for the last, and hardest, leg of her journey, before she pulled back out on the highway.

No cars had passed. At least that hadn't changed. Raspberry Ridge was a beautiful little gem that not very many people knew about. If tourists knew, they would flock here, although they'd have to find a different place to stay, since the old inn had long ago shut down, although Shannon could remember pieces of it from her childhood.

Still, that was more than forty years ago, and so much had changed. So much. She tried to push those thoughts aside. Change wasn't necessarily bad, but it was easier to swallow in small doses.

She was face-to-face with the fact that because she hadn't been there for almost twenty years and had decided to come back to live without visiting first, she was going to have a lot of big doses of change.

Her car moved slowly down the highway, as though she wanted to put off the inevitable for as long as she could, but soon the first houses of Raspberry Ridge came into view. The same, yet different. Older, more paint chips, more weather-beaten. They'd been through almost twenty Michigan winters, which was no small thing, especially along the lake.

Winter had always been fun to her, lots of snow, lots of things to do —skiing and sledding and building snow forts and castles and playing with her children in it, even ice-skating at times. Winter had been her favorite time of the year, and she'd always been a little disappointed when the snow had melted and spring had sprung.

Not that she didn't love Michigan springs and summers as well. Fall was maybe her least favorite time, but it held the promise of another winter coming.

Now that she was older, the cold got to her more, the wind felt chillier. Her coats and winter clothing didn't keep the chill out like they used to. Maybe she would hate winter. Maybe this was a big mistake. Maybe she should have gone to Florida.

She kept puttering along. There was the church on the hill. The old one that had closed before she had left and before the new one closer to the lake had opened. That's where the grave was. The one she hadn't visited in almost twenty years. What kind of mother was she to have not visited her daughter's grave in all that time?

She felt guilt clogging up her throat, but she pushed it down. Forcefully. After all, she had taken the absolute very best care of her daughter while she had been alive. She had been the very best mother that she could possibly be. Who cared whether she took care of the grave after her death?

Suddenly she had an urgent need to see it. But she was already past the place where she needed to pull off, and she kept going.

There, at the end of the dead-end street, she could see the healing garden that had taken the place of the old gazebo that had sat there all through her childhood. It had started to decay and fall, and the town had demolished it before her children had been old enough to hang out there like she and her friends had.

They had had so much fun sitting in the gazebo, talking, making plans, using it as a meeting point for a trip to the pebble beach.

So many memories, and yet the gazebo was long gone.

She turned her head and saw Fran's store.

Almost without thinking, her hands turned the wheel, and she pulled in along the street, parking right in front of the store that didn't seem to have changed at all since the day Shannon had left. She had stopped here and bought a soda and a bag of chips for both of her children. They had been a good bit younger than Yolanda at eight and ten, and she hadn't wanted to have a whole lot of questions, she hadn't wanted to have to talk to them. So, she convinced her husband to stop, and she'd run in and gotten them what amounted to bribes to stay quiet for the trip to Detroit.

James hadn't wanted to stop, not when they were just getting started, but she insisted.

She couldn't even think about James, so she put those memories aside to think about later too. It seemed like that was what she did with everything her whole life, set it aside until she was able to handle it. When would she be able? Here she was, fifty years old, and still didn't feel like she was adult enough to face all the pain and heartbreak in her past.

But she definitely couldn't think about that now. Not if she was going to go into Fran's, which apparently she was since she had parked the car right in front of the store.

Part of her wanted to go in, to see what had changed, and part of her wanted to run in the other direction.

Deliberately putting her hand on the latch and yanking hard, she opened her door and stepped out, adjusting her purse over her shoulder and squinting in the bright sunlight. She adjusted her shades and closed the door, walking with determined steps to Holloway's General Store.

The bell jangled over her head as she opened the door and stepped in. It wasn't hard to recognize Fran, who was adjusting some candy on a shelf right in front of the checkout counter. Her hair was white, and there were definitely added pounds, which gave her figure a more matronly look than what Shannon remembered, but Fran wasn't the only one who had a more matronly look.

She didn't look like she was in her twenties anymore either. Although, she had been thirty-four when they left. With three children, she'd been slender, maybe not teenage slender, but she definitely didn't have the matronly figure that many mothers of three did. Not then anyway. She'd gained weight since the divorce, although she lost it before it had been finalized. Sleepless nights, wishing she could have done something to keep her family together, wondering what she could have done to prevent her husband's infidelity, and constantly trying to tell herself that she had done the best she could, and there was no point in looking back.

Fran straightened and turned around. She blinked and then tilted her head as Shannon removed her sunglasses.

Shannon didn't really expect Fran to remember her. It had been almost twenty years.

"Shannon McKay, well, I'll be… I guess it's not McKay anymore, is it?"

"Actually, it is McKay." That had been the first thing she'd done after her divorce was final. If James didn't want her anymore, she wasn't going to keep his name. Her kids had been a little upset with her. They hadn't wanted to have a name that was different than hers, but they hadn't wanted to ditch their father's name either, and she had not encouraged that. She had gently suggested that the name that they were born with was the name that they identified with. She encouraged them to not do anything rash. After all, James had been a good father. If by good, one ignored the fact that he had cheated on his wife and broken up his family, committing adultery and leaving a wake of pain and devastation behind him.

Fran's face fell, and her brows lowered. "Oh? I hadn't heard."

The gossip hadn't reached Raspberry Ridge? Shannon supposed that made sense. After all, she didn't have any ties left in Raspberry Ridge. Both of her parents had passed on in the last five years, and her siblings had long since fled. She stayed in touch with them but not on a daily basis. It was more like she picked up the phone for Thanksgiving or Christmas or maybe texted them on their birthday. And they did the same for her.

She nodded.

"I'm sorry to hear that," Fran said, sounding truly sorry as she bustled forward, her arms outstretched. And if her walk was a little bit less steady than it used to be, if she seemed a little bit more frail, Shannon ignored it as she allowed the older woman to wrap her arms around her and envelop her in a cinnamon-scented hug.

It felt like home.

Without thought, she felt herself hugging back, tightly, the kind of hug a person gave someone they knew and loved and missed.

"I'm sorry I mentioned it," Fran said, stepping back and looking up at Shannon, almost as though she was hungry for a good look at her.

"It was amicable." She didn't feel like she was lying when she said that. Her husband and she were still talking. She could call him up today, he would answer her call, and they would have a civil conversation. However, she knew there was a part of her that resented what he did, that was hurt in a way words couldn't explain over the fact that he had walked out on their almost thirty-year marriage. That he had obviously not even tried to make things right between them. He hadn't suggested counseling, hadn't even told her that there was anything wrong. She just intercepted a text his girlfriend had sent, and he'd come clean about everything and moved out that same day.

"Well, that's good to hear. So many times, there's so much fighting and bickering that the lawyers get everything and a person has to be careful about what they say." Fran waved her hand. "But Raspberry Ridge seems to be the place for second chances lately. You wouldn't believe the people who have come back and found love here. It's...been good for my old heart to watch."

"That's not going to happen to me. But I am back to stay."

"You are? Are you looking for a place to rent?" Fran asked, and Shannon figured that if she was, Fran would certainly know of the places that were available.

But she wasn't.

She thought about hedging or dodging the question, but there was no point. Raspberry Ridge was a small town, and everyone was going to know sooner or later. It might as well be now.

"No. I bought the old inn."

Fran froze, her eyes opening wide in shock. "That was you?"

Shannon nodded. She had set up an LLC and bought it under that, not necessarily to keep the townspeople from knowing that it was her, although it had that effect as well. But it was more for tax purposes. Her accountant had suggested that was the way she should go.

"Well, I'll be," Fran said, a hand going to her heart. "I can't believe it." She huffed out a breath. "Mind you, I'm happy about it, because having that old inn opened up, fixed up, generating revenue, and bringing people in could be nothing but good for this town. But... I would never have guessed that it would have been you."

Shannon nodded. She didn't want to go into the whole divorce and her needing to have something to do, a purpose in life. She felt worthless, with her kids gone and her husband gone and her rattling around that big old house in the 'burbs of Detroit by herself. The one that held all the memories of her raising her children and their laughter ringing in the walls, the late nights she'd spent staying up with them holding them while they were feverish or coughing, the times James had come home with good news from work, a raise, a vacation, and just the regular old family time around the table in the evening as they ate supper together.

All of it was there, crumbling in on her, crushing her, making it so that she could barely breathe. She needed a new start. But she didn't want to do something completely new, like move to Florida. She needed a new start in an old spot, one that was familiar and welcoming and one where she knew she could heal.

Raspberry Ridge was the only place that could happen. And what better thing to do than to fix up the old inn? It would be new, yet it was old at the same time. It was in her memory, but the memories weren't so personal that she couldn't handle the pain. After all, if she tried to move back into the house that they'd owned when Yolanda had died, she wouldn't have been able to handle it.

Thankfully, that house was not along the main street, and she hadn't seen it coming in. If she didn't want to, she wouldn't have to see it at all. Because she would have to make a concerted effort to pull into the driveway and drive back to the house. And then it would be a little awkward as she sat there while the owners wondered what in the world the crazy woman was doing staring at their house.

Yeah, that wasn't going to happen.

"So are you just here scoping it out? How long are you staying?"

"I'm here for good."

She didn't elaborate, and Fran looked a little confused. Shannon knew that wasn't the way people usually operated.

"Oh my goodness. And James... James isn't with you?"

Shannon shook her head. She knew that Fran was just digging for information, but she didn't feel ready to share that, even though she wasn't trying to hide anything. She wasn't the one who had done anything wrong.

"It's been a long drive, and I'm here for some coffee. Do you have some?" she asked, although she could smell it when she walked in.

Fran nodded and pointed at the coffee machine that sat at the end of the checkout counter.

Shannon walked up and got herself a cup as Fran chattered about the changes that had been happening in Raspberry Ridge since she had left. She also talked about some of the things that hadn't changed a bit.

Shannon paid for her coffee, and then she escaped out of the store without giving out any more personal information. People were going to find out eventually. It was a small town, and that's what happened in small towns, but it didn't have to be today. She had a little bit more time to herself before she had to share more of her life with the world, or with Raspberry Ridge, which was the world when one lived in a small town.

She took two steps toward her vehicle before the sight of the healing garden caught her eye.

On a whim, she turned and walked the fifty yards to the entrance. She had heard via an article in the local paper that Raspberry Ridge had put in a healing garden. The article had been more about Dominic and Vera Miller, the award-winning duo who had built the garden, than it had been about Raspberry Ridge, but the setting had been what had caught Shannon's eye.

And now, as she read the plaque that was visible from the gate, she remembered that the article had said that Dominic and Vera had lost a child.

To those who are waiting in heaven for us.
This is a place where we can sit and remember, wish you were still with us,
be happy for your good fortune, and look forward to the day when we are
reunited.

She didn't remember reading about the plaque in the paper and wondered if maybe it had been added later.

The words were perfect though. Because Yolanda waited in heaven, and since the day of her death, Shannon had been looking for a way to heal and had been looking forward to them meeting again.

This was definitely a place she wanted to get back to. But as she saw the sun lowering in the sky, she knew she had to move on. She didn't know what she was going to find when she got to the inn, and she needed to face that for sure.

With one last look at the plaque and then the healing garden in general, she turned and walked back to her car.

In some ways, this had been harder than what she thought, and in some ways, she felt stronger just for what she'd been able to accomplish, coming to town, walking into Fran's and chatting, and seeing that the town was just as welcoming as it always had been. And then, knowing there was someone else who shared her grief and sorrow and who had gotten through it, using that grief to do something to be a blessing to other people.

Maybe that was what Shannon was doing with the inn, using her grief and the heartache that she had endured to be a blessing to others. The thought made her smile.

Had she lost her mind?

The possibility was very real, Shannon had to admit as she stood staring up at what used to be a building full of grandeur and prestige but now was just a crumbling old structure.

The porch dipped and swayed, the shutters hung crooked or were completely gone, and the spouting swayed in the wind, grating against the brick.

It looked like it needed a new roof and about one million other things that were all running around her head, adding up the dollar signs.

She'd bought the property sight unseen three weeks prior when her divorce settlement had finally hit her bank account. Their house was sold, all the possessions divided, and she had gotten her half.

It had been a bad day, because that really made it real.

It was final. She was divorced. The life she had built from the time she had gotten married was completely gone. Years and years of what she thought was going to be a lifetime love and a family that stood the test of time was no longer. It maybe wasn't worse than the day of the tragedy, but it was close.

She'd been scrolling the internet, looking for properties because she needed somewhere to go.

Raspberry Ridge called her name, but the only place she saw for sale there was the old inn. She couldn't click on it fast enough, and surprisingly, when she called the number for the realtor, she got a live person on the phone. At the time, she thought it was a gift from the Lord, but now... She didn't really think something like this would come from God. Something that was so broken and old and run down that the best, most efficient solution was almost certainly to bulldoze it.

It was the way her life felt. The most effective solution to solve all of her problems would be to bulldoze everything. Was there anything in her life worth salvaging?

Of course, her children. She wouldn't give them up for anything, but...they were on their own. They didn't need her. And they didn't necessarily want her.

She tried not to feel bad about that. After all, she'd wanted to raise them to be independent and self-supporting. She didn't want them to be dependent on her, or the government, or anyone other than the Lord, in order for them to live their lives.

She'd probably been more successful than what she wanted to be, because they definitely were doing well, which made her happy, but they didn't need her either. And that was a little bit hard. She wanted someone to need her.

Her husband didn't, her kids didn't, and...this old house... It was too much like her for her to be able to do anything with it.

She turned around, looking out at the gorgeous views of Lake Michigan. That was one of the best things about this place—the views. From every single window on the west side, a person could see the absolutely stunning majesty of the lake in the distance.

Whoever built the inn put it in a perfect spot.

She wrapped her arms around her waist and looked at the changing sky as the sun sank lower.

She'd been staring off into space for she didn't know how long when the sound of a motor brought her attention back to the present.

It must be Dominic Miller, she thought to herself as a pickup pulled into the cracked and broken but previously paved lot and stopped beside her car.

The large truck had a ladder strapped to the top of it and the kind of bed in the back that contained a myriad of tools.

Dominic had told her that he used to only do landscaping construction, but he'd branched off into residential and commercial building construction in order to be able to stay closer to home since he and his wife had children.

She liked that. A family man. A man who put his wife and kids first. Who built his business around them, instead of raising his family around his business.

She turned and started walking toward the pickup. Dominic had gotten out, and they met about ten yards away from his truck.

She stuck her hand out. "I'm Shannon McKay. You must be Dominic."

"I am. Dominic Miller. Here to take a look at the inn for you. And wow, do you have your work cut out for you."

Her heart sank. She thought maybe he would say something encouraging like "this is going to be a gorgeous place once we're done with it," or "the bones here are amazing, and it won't take too much to dust it up into something really nice." Kind of along the lines of what the realtor had said as she spoke to her late at night. Although, the realtor hadn't had to do too much selling. It was the only property available in Raspberry Ridge, and she was going to purchase it, no matter what.

"Yeah. The pictures certainly didn't do the devastation justice," she said, trying to induce some levity into her tone.

"Yeah, I don't know what you saw, but maybe the pics were doctored on the internet. Sometimes that happens. Although I do believe that's illegal for real estate agencies to do."

"If it's not, it should be," she said. But she felt like she had to be honest. "I didn't see any doctored pictures though. I just wanted the inn, and no one could have talked me out of it."

Dominic raised his brows and nodded, lifting his eyes to the big building in front of them. "She is grand, isn't she?"

"I vaguely remember in my childhood it being a bustling place. But even then, it was slightly derelict. I remember my parents saying it would be nice if someone would restore it to its former glory. I think they remembered it when it was really something to see."

"I think there are some pictures in the Blueberry Beach library of it in its glory days. That's probably something you might wanna look up if you're interested in restoring it to a similar state."

"I'll keep that in mind. I don't know that I want to be historically accurate as much as I want to be financially responsible as well as paying close attention to safety and also modern conveniences. People aren't going to want to use outhouses."

"I don't know whether every room would have an attached bathroom or not. I suppose that's something we're here to see, right?"

"That's right," she said as she dug the key out of her purse. "Shall we?" she asked, holding it up.

He took it from her, and they walked to the front door. She had no idea which door the key actually worked for or if it was even locked.

As though reading her mind, Dominic tried the doorknob before he even put the key in the lock. It turned easily in his hand.

"Looks to me like this was just for show," he said, holding up the key with a little smile.

Shannon smiled back, but a part of her was concerned. She was planning on sleeping here. This was where she was going to live. If there were no locks... But the place was quiet, deserted, hardly the place where gangsters or worse might hang out. In fact, if she were running from something, this would be the perfect place.

"Do you know if the electricity is on?" Dominic asked as he stepped inside.

"It's supposed to be," she said, hitting the switch on the side but not holding her breath that the lights were actually going to go on. The way the place looked on the outside, she really did think it might be better if they just bulldozed the whole thing.

To her surprise, the lights worked.

"Wow. That is a pleasant surprise," she said. She couldn't keep the relief and excitement out of her voice. She needed some kind of lift, and the electricity provided it. Sometimes a person just got so down that one more thing was going to be the last thing they could handle, and she felt like she was almost at that point. The electricity shot her up a few notches, so she felt like maybe she could take a little more before she quit.

But what did quitting look like? She didn't even know. She didn't have anything to quit to. Everything that she loved had been taken from her or else left, although it wasn't fair to categorize her children like that. They were doing what kids were supposed to do, weren't they?

It was a good thing the electricity worked, and she had that lift, because as they walked through the building, there wasn't much to recommend it. Walls were peeling, everything needed to be painted, most of the lights were out, even though the electricity was on, and on the north wing of the house, it looked like perhaps there was even a water leak.

By the time she and Dominic had finished walking through it and had come back to the kitchen, which was probably the room that needed the least amount of attention, she was feeling very despondent.

"I have to ask, are you sure about this?" Dominic said as they walked into the kitchen and stopped at the island.

She put her purse on it and looked up at him.

"I'm just asking because this is a lot of work. It's going to take a ton of money. You're going to have something amazing when we're done, but... The time and the work and the money... You're looking at at least a year probably. You might be able to open it a little bit at a time, but it's going to be a year before everything is done."

That wasn't what she wanted to hear. Although, the part of her that really wanted to be successful, to recover from the tragedy that had been her life so far, and to actually build something worth having said yes, absolutely, she could do this.

"So you think it's too much?" she asked, looking at him steadily. She could handle it if he said yes. It was his professional opinion, and while she might get a second opinion, she wasn't going to discount what the man said. He did this for a living.

"There's endless potential here. It's a historic property, and it's perfect for someone who believes in second chances."

Shannon blinked. She wasn't expecting him to go there. That was almost word for word what the description had said on the real estate website.

"My wife, Vera, always says that broken things can be made more beautiful than they ever were before. If you look at our lives, we lost our son, and we almost lost each other, and now our marriage and our family is more than I ever dreamed it could be. Sometimes I think Vera is prophetic, because she's right. Sometimes something has to be broken before it can be made whole, if that makes sense."

"You're starting to sound like a poet, and I wasn't expecting that from my contractor."

Dominic grinned, a little self-effacing. "You can blame my wife. She's the reason for all the goodness in my life. Along with the Lord."

"I think she's wise."

"If you're really interested in doing this, you might want to talk to my wife about the design inside. I think she would cut you a pretty good break. She specializes in healing spaces, and that seems to be like something you might be interested in."

Shannon wanted to smile and agree with him, but she felt her defenses going up. She didn't want to be that vulnerable with anyone, let alone a complete stranger. Someone she was going to have to see every day for the next year if his estimations were correct.

"I'll think about it," she said, and her words came out very cool, very standoffish, very much protecting herself from any kind of vulnerability.

Dominic didn't seem to notice or mind. "It's gonna be kind of hard to get you a quote for the entire building, but if you don't mind going piece by piece, I can give you some ideas and some quotes to get started."

Dominic went on to say that he felt like they should do a thorough inspection of the foundation and the bones of the building and mentioned some other things while Shannon listened, feeling bad that she had been so cool when he had been so open and vulnerable with her. He'd admitted that he'd almost lost his wife, and she wished that she knew more about that. Not that it would do her any good now. Her husband wasn't interested in coming back, and she wasn't even sure she wanted him. Did she really want someone who cheated? And honestly, once she got over the sadness of seeing everything that she had built get torn to shreds, she knew that she hadn't married the best man anyway. The best man had stayed in Raspberry Ridge, and she hadn't seen him in decades.

Dominic got her contact information and promised to send an estimate over in a reasonable amount of time. Then he left, and Shannon wandered back down to the once grand entranceway to stand at the top of the stairs and watch the sunset.

Everything she owned was in the back of her SUV and behind her in this building. This was what she was staking the rest of her life on. She had a little bit of cash coming from the sale of a few other things that had taken a bit longer to arrange, and she wondered if maybe she was being crazy for spending it all on fixing this up. But there was a part of her that already knew that it was what she was going to do no matter what. Maybe it was foolish, maybe it was crazy, maybe she was just reacting out of depression and desperation, but this was where she was going to settle, and this was where she was going to build the rest of her life. At this inn.

And it wasn't just going to be Dominic and his crew and whatever subcontractors he hired. He'd mumbled about all of that stuff, but Shannon had done her share of painting at least, and she had done some DIY projects around the house over the years. She enjoyed working with her hands. Maybe it wouldn't cost as much as what Dominic was thinking, because she would pitch in and do everything she could to bring this old place back to its former glory.

And maybe, somewhere along the way, she would heal herself while she was at it.

But as she watched the sun slowly sinking past the edge of the lake, she realized that it wasn't just about herself, and it wasn't just about the building either.

In her mind, she could see families, smiling and laughing, coming up the stairs. Couples finding romance, maybe a second chance, like she would like to have had, or maybe couples who made the right decision the first time. Laughter and dancing, and smiling faces and people being enveloped by the inn and by its charm and its stately grandeur, giving them a restful place from the world.

Maybe it wasn't just about restoration, maybe it was about looking beyond herself and creating a place where other people could find joy and happiness, and maybe even some healing as well.

Three

❧

The next morning, Shannon decided before she could even begin to tackle anything in the inn, she needed coffee and normalcy. She was tempted to jump in her car—it would be quicker—but the late September breeze was warm, and part of the reason she moved back to Raspberry Ridge was because she missed the fresh, wholesome air that came in off the lake. Plus, she missed the community that formed around her and the small-town vibes. As much as that made her nervous and defensive as well.

Regardless, she was determined to enjoy the day, so she grabbed a light jacket and stepped out into the bright September sunlight. The air was clean and fresh and seemed to make its way to the depths of her lungs as she took in a deep breath, closing her eyes and smiling at how good it felt.

The walk to town was only ten minutes or so, and it did her body good to limber up.

She'd slept on a bed, using sheets that she had brought to make it so it was clean. She didn't want to know how many spiders were in the room with her, but at least she knew there were none in the sheets when she put them on the bed.

Today would consist of a long laundry list of trying to make sure that she got the basic necessities that she would need in order to live there figured out before she even began to tackle the things she needed to do at the inn to get it ready for guests. Maybe Dominic's estimate would come in and it would be well below what she was afraid it was going to be.

But she didn't need any of that now. She just needed coffee and maybe some food.

The scent of cinnamon wafted through the air, feeling like a hug as she looked closer at the bakery her friend had run when she lived in Raspberry Ridge.

She couldn't remember her name, but she remembered Lauren, who had been Yolanda's friend, although she hadn't been there the day of the tragedy.

Still, that had been forever ago, and the cinnamon smell drew her right in. The bells jingled above her head as the door closed behind her. A woman in her late twenties stood up from behind the counter.

"Lauren?" she said carefully.

"Mrs. Callahan?" Lauren said tentatively.

"It's McKay, but you're right. I'm Yolanda's mother." She stumbled over the name of her daughter, and she wondered if it was even wise to say anything when she saw Lauren's eyes flicker. In order to get past the awkward moment, she continued to talk. "I bought the inn, the Sunset Inn on the hill. I'm planning on restoring it."

Almost as though Lauren sensed Shannon's nervousness, her uncertainty, or maybe just how difficult the last year had been for her, she smiled warmly. "I have fresh apple cider donuts, and they're on the house. Especially for anyone brave enough to take on the old inn. That would be amazing if you're able to fix it up and have guests. That's your plan?" she said, bustling around behind the counter, getting a plate, and setting two steaming donuts on top of it. They glistened with a sugary glaze as Lauren looked up. "Coffee?"

"Please," Shannon said. "And I can pay for it."

"I'll charge you for the coffee, but the donuts are on the house. This is a new recipe, and I'm trying to get opinions on it."

"Well, they smell delicious, if that counts for anything," Shannon said. She remembered Lauren as being slightly serious but always down for a good time. She'd been one of Yolanda's best friends, and she'd spent a lot of time at Shannon's house. It felt like she had grown up, though, and was more of an equal to Shannon than a little girl—like there weren't two decades between them.

"I'm so glad you're back in town."

"It's good to be back."

"When did you get in?" Lauren asked.

"Just yesterday. I slept in the inn last night, but it needs a lot of work. I don't really want to spend another night lying in bed, wondering how many eight-legged visitors are in the room with me."

Lauren laughed with her and then set the coffee down on the counter and rang it up.

It wasn't that much, and Shannon felt a little bad taking the donuts for free, but Lauren had insisted.

"I see my wife is using you as a guinea pig," a deep voice said as Lauren finished running Shannon's card.

"Ms. McKay, this is my husband, Cannon."

"You can call me Shannon. You're old enough to have children of your own."

"And we do," Lauren said with a smile.

"I almost lost her and the kids, but there's something special about this town. If you're coming in for a second chance, it seems to be conducive to that." Cannon had put an arm around Lauren's shoulder, and Lauren looked up at him like he hung the moon and stars.

"I'm glad things worked out for the two of you," Shannon said sincerely, and just as sincerely, she wished they had worked out for her.

"You can't do it by yourself, though," Lauren said, biting her lip as though guessing Shannon's problem. "Both of you have to be on board with it."

"Yes," she said, saying nothing more. Instead, for lack of something to do with her hands, she reached for a donut and took a bite.

It was buttery soft and sweet with just the right amount of apple cider tanginess to make it burst on her tongue.

"Oh my goodness," she said, a little embarrassed because her mouth was full, but she just couldn't help herself. "This is amazing." She didn't think she'd ever eaten anything like it. "I'm not sure if it's the texture, the sugar versus just enough of a tangy taste to make it interesting, or the scent that just seems to permeate everything that makes it amazing. Whatever you did, keep this recipe."

Lauren laughed. And Cannon said, "I told you so." He shook his head and looked at Shannon. "Lauren's always afraid that her stuff isn't good enough. I keep telling her she's the best baker on the lake, but she just doesn't believe me."

"That would include Chicago, and I know there are places in Chicago that I just can't compare to."

"I have to respectfully disagree," Shannon said. She had lived in Detroit, but it wasn't like she'd never been to Chicago. And she definitely had never tasted anything like this there.

"Well, it's good to know. Your vote has been duly taken into consideration." Lauren grinned.

Shannon couldn't answer, because she had taken another big bite. She really was thinking about getting a dozen donuts to take home with her, trying to convince herself that she really needed food to survive. Which was true, but she didn't need to eat donuts all day. She didn't come here in order to gain enough winter fat to be mistaken for a bear come spring.

"I'm glad you're back in town. Grace and Claire are both back as well, and I bet that both of them would like to meet with you. I think it would provide some closure for us, if you're ever willing."

"I definitely think that would be something that we could do in the future. Let me get my sea legs under me first. I have some things I need to do at the inn." Shannon wasn't sure how she felt about that. Maybe talking to the girls would bring some closure, if not for her, for them. Maybe it would be good for her as well though. To know exactly what happened. At the time, she'd been devastated, upset, and had tried not to blame anyone, to place blame where it didn't belong. And then, she'd been so eager to get out of town, it hadn't occurred to her that the girls might need to talk to her.

"I ran from it for a long time. I think Grace and Claire did too. It wasn't nearly as bad once we stopped running and talked to each other."

Shannon didn't answer. She truly did have a donut in her mouth, but she didn't know what to say to that either. It seemed like she had spent a lot of her adult life running. She'd run from Raspberry Ridge after the tragedy, and now she was running from Detroit after her husband left and her kids had scattered.

"I don't want to run. In fact, I think my new mantra is I need to stand and face everything."

"It's okay to be vulnerable too. I needed to learn that lesson when Cannon and I went through what we did. I thought I could stand on my own and I didn't need anyone else, and he proved me wrong."

"That's an awfully nice way to put it," Cannon said, giving his wife a kiss on the top of the head before moving away from her. "I was working too much. That was the bottom line. I'm glad Lauren gave me a wake-up call. Because we've been happier now than we ever were before. Sometimes it just takes a little bit of reevaluation in your life to figure out where it's off track and how to get it back."

Shannon nodded. "I guess I'm reevaluating my life right now." That was all she was going to say. Lauren was probably right about being vulnerable, but sometimes a person had to work up to that. She wasn't ready to share everything with people that she barely knew. Plus, she didn't even know if she was able to be honest with herself yet.

She took the coffee and wrapped up the second donut.

"I can give you a bag for that," Lauren offered.

"That would be wonderful if you would. I need to stop at the hardware store."

"It'll be a pleasant surprise to find out that Lance has taken over the hardware store from his dad. It's great to know that some things never change."

Shannon's heart flipped and sank at the mention of Lance. She hadn't been allowing herself to think of him at all. She had kind of been hoping that he had finally left town and she wouldn't have to face him.

"That's nice," she said, knowing her tone sounded like it was anything but.

"I know, isn't it?" Lauren said, completely missing Shannon's discomfort. "It's so comforting to know that some things never change. That's one of the reasons why it was so nice to be able to open up

Mom's bakeshop again. I know that she would love to know that I'm here with my family, but it's also just nice for people who come to town to see that the store is still here, that some things stand the test of time, you know?" She smiled at her husband, who gave her one last grin before he disappeared into the back.

Shannon's marriage hadn't stood the test of time, but it was like Lauren had just said, it took two. She had wanted to put the work in. She would have been willing, if her husband had let her know that there was any kind of problem. But it hadn't been like that—he'd found someone else that he wanted more than her, and by the time she found out about it, he was already so deep in a relationship that he hadn't wanted to let the other woman go. So it was Shannon who had been let go.

The bell over the door rang, and more customers walked in. Shannon slipped out, giving Lauren a wave and letting her know that she would be back again. Definitely. Those apple cider donuts were addicting, she was afraid.

At least she'd resisted the temptation to buy a dozen anyway.

She calculated in her mind how much time it would take if she just walked back to the inn, got her car, and then drove to Blueberry Beach to see if they had a hardware store. She was pretty sure they did. Maybe there was even one in Strawberry Sands and she wouldn't have to go quite that far, but that was just her being silly. Why would she get in her car and drive to a different town when she could walk to the store next door?

She knew the answer—she would do it just to avoid Lance.

But she wasn't such a fool as to think that she could live in Raspberry Ridge and avoid Lance forever, so, dredging up what little nerve she had left, she walked a few steps down the street to the hardware store and opened the door.

She wished she hadn't opened it with quite such force, because the bells seemed to clang and jangle above her in extra loud tones.

It still sounded the same way it did decades ago when his dad ran the shop. She remembered trying to think of excuses to go to the hardware store back then, just in case Lance was working the counter after school.

Lance—a man, it had to be Lance—looked up from helping another customer. Shannon had heard the phrase "time stood still," but she never really experienced it before.

She definitely experienced it then. It was Lance. Same kind eyes, same strong nose, same tanned face, although maybe just a little older, a little more weather-beaten, and there was silver lacing his hair now.

"Shannon?" There were decades of questions in his tone.

She had forgotten to breathe, and her lungs screamed at her just in time as the edges of her vision grew black. She sucked in a breath.

"Lance," she said, wishing her tone sounded normal but knowing it didn't.

She cleared her throat and tried again. "It's been a long time."

"Too long," he said, his eyes narrowing, and there were still questions in his tone. It was like he had forgotten the customer in front of him. She wandered off, maybe knowing that whatever was going on between Lance and Shannon deserved to happen without interruption.

"How are you?" he asked, and there was definitely concern and caring in his voice. He'd always been sweet and kind, even as a teen. He'd been extra considerate and one of the best people she knew, man or woman. She had no idea why she had turned him down and chosen James. No idea. She had been a fool.

But true to form, Lance didn't seem angry, and he wasn't carrying a grudge.

"I've been well." She figured that was the truth. She hadn't been good—she'd actually been pretty bad, considering all the things that had happened to her—but she hadn't been sick, so her words were true.

They were still staring at each other, and with the presence of the other customers in the store, Shannon felt like she needed to say something.

"So you took over your dad's store?"

He nodded. "They passed away, and Katie needed me, so I stayed here." He looked like he might have been going to say something more, but he didn't.

"Are you back to stay?" he asked, and it seemed like there might have been hope in his voice. But that was ridiculous. There couldn't have been. Their relationship, what it was, was long ago, and he couldn't still be holding a torch for her.

She was tempted to ask if he was married, but instead she looked at his ring finger—his bare ring finger—as she answered him. "Yes. I'm staying here for the rest of my life. I bought the old inn."

"The Sunset Inn?" he asked, sounding shocked.

"The very one," she said, wondering if, like some men, he didn't wear a ring because there was a danger of it getting caught in machinery. After all, he ran a hardware store, but... The only machinery he ran was the cash register, right?

Why did it matter to her whether he wore a ring or not? She wasn't interested in a relationship. None. After all, she thought James was going to be true to her, and he wasn't. She wasn't going to go down that road again. She wasn't going to give some man the power over her to hurt her in any way. That was just not in the cards for her, just like moving out of this town was not in the cards for her. She was back to stay.

"I'm happy to hear that."

They didn't say anything else, because she didn't know what to say. Finally, she took a breath and looked around the store. "Well, I have a few things I need to get."

He jerked his head and said, "I can help you. Just let me know."

The words made her feel like he was talking about more than just shopping in the store today, but he didn't say anything more, and she wandered away from him. She could hear voices murmuring, and his deep voice saying something, as she picked up a few things that she knew she was going to need that day. She was going to have to take stock of her money, figuring out how much she was going to be able to spend for repairs and trying to figure out whether she would be able to open a part of the inn to house guests to maybe start earning some money so she would be able to afford to fix the rest of it up.

So much she didn't know. Why had she done this on the spur of the moment?

But she knew the answer. She was desperate to return to the town of her youth. And this was the only way.

She finally had gathered up what she needed, managing to avoid Lance in the process, and took the things to the cash register.

He rang them up and set them in a bag. She paid with a card, and as he handed her receipt back along with her card, their fingers brushed.

She tried to ignore the surge of electricity that ran through the tips of her fingers, tingling down her arm.

"It's good to see you, Shannon. Really good."

Her heart beat hard as she mumbled something—she wasn't even sure what—and turned and fled out the door.

Four

Shannon sat in the small room off the kitchen that she assumed had once been a caretaker's room. It had a small bed and a dresser. The bathroom that was just off to the side was the nicest bathroom in the hotel. It was still run down and needed a facelift, but it was the one that she was going to use, and it would work for now. Nothing leaked, and she had used some of the cleaner she had bought at the hardware store to get some of the grime off. It didn't feel too bad.

But now, she had to make some hard phone calls.

Pressing the button on her phone, she waited for it to ring and the camera to show the picture of her oldest child, Alex. He was twenty-six years old and pragmatic like his father.

"Mom!" He answered the phone, obviously in the middle of a run, since he was sweaty and standing on some kind of bike path.

"Alex. How are you?"

"I'm doing good. I expected to hear from you before this, though."

"You can call me," she said, and she tried to keep any kind of motherly discipline out of her voice. But it was true. Alex never called her. Although he always answered when she called.

"You're right. Still, you got into town what? Two days ago? How are you?"

"I'm doing just fine. I've been busy. And I just got in yesterday."

"Okay. What is that in the background? You're staying there?" He lifted the phone to his face and scrunched his eyes as though trying to make out exactly what was going on behind her. If she had been thinking, she would have made the call from the kitchen. It was the nicest room in the inn.

"This is the inn I bought."

The phone moved back away from his face as he digested her words.

"You bought an inn?" he asked, and it was obvious from his tone that he was trying to reconcile his mother with the sentence that she had uttered, and was finding it difficult.

"Yes. In Raspberry Ridge, the town you were born in."

"The one you never talk about."

She lifted her head in a regal nod. She still didn't want to talk about it. Not really. Especially not the reason she left. Not with Alex. He was old enough to remember his sister and the pain the tragedy had caused.

"Because that's where Yolanda died. You moved back there?"

Thankfully, he didn't go into it, although she wondered if maybe he needed to. He was a man, and his emotions were definitely not worn on his sleeve.

"Yes. Into the inn."

"Which you bought," he said, but it sounded like a question.

"That's correct."

"Mom, are you having some kind of midlife crisis or something?"

"I don't think I'm the one who's having the midlife crisis," she said, offended by that question.

"If I recall correctly, it was run down back when we lived there. Did someone else buy it and fix it up and you purchased it from them?"

"No. I'm fixing it up."

"Is that wise? Do you have the financial resources to do that? I know you got a bit of a windfall from the divorce settlement, but... That has to last you the rest of your life, unless you're going to get a job and go back into the workforce, which of course you can if you want to." He paused for a moment. "You could go back to school and get a degree, do whatever it is you've always wanted to do."

"I always wanted to live in Raspberry Ridge, and I want to own an inn. I want to fix it up. I want to make a place where people come and are happy."

That should answer all of his questions, although probably not satisfactorily if she knew Alex.

"Mother. I'm a little concerned about you. This is...not like you at all. You're the cautious one. The one who doesn't take unnecessary risks."

"The one who's faithful. The one who doesn't cheat. The one who does what she says she's going to do, no matter how hard it is." She probably shouldn't have said that, but it was the truth. And she just wanted to remind him that there were reasons why she was doing what she was doing, and they weren't of her choosing. If she had her choice, she and her husband would still be married, although... Knowing what she knew about him now, she really didn't want to stay married to him.

"All right. I hear you. Well, you know I'm here if you need anything."

"I know." He had just finished law school and started practicing law in the last year. He had gotten married in his last year of law school, and not only did he have his school bills to pay, but he was setting up a home for his future family, since his wife was now expecting their first child. She would have to be really hard up before she would ask Alex for help with anything.

"Is your car running okay?" he asked, which she almost laughed about. Her car was the least of her worries.

"It's only a year old. If anything happens to it, it's under warranty." That was one good thing about her husband—he had an excellent job as a lawyer, and he'd been very generous with his money. She didn't want for anything.

The settlement that she'd gotten was because of the hard work that he had put in. Although she had made sure that he was comfortable at home, and he had wanted for nothing once he set foot in the house. Their home had been an oasis of love and laughter and family and calm and peace. She had made sure of it, because of the stress of his job. Would he have been able to be successful without her? She thought not, since she had worked as a waitress to help put him through law school.

Regardless, it didn't matter now. She had been with him, and she had gotten half of everything, which he hadn't even seemed to think about. He was so desperate to be with his new love that he didn't care how much it cost him.

That had hurt probably as much as anything.

"All right, Mom. You take care, okay?"

"I will. I love you."

"I love you too."

She swiped off and breathed a sigh of relief. That wasn't as hard as what she thought it was going to be. And the hard phone call was over. He might have questions, he might continue to question her sanity, but she broke the ice, and now he knew.

Now, she just needed to call Emma before Alex told Emma what was going on.

Emma had just graduated from college that spring. She had started her first job in Ann Arbor, and Shannon hadn't seen her since June.

Maybe part of the reason that Shannon wanted to move to Raspberry Ridge was because it was closer to her daughter than Detroit.

That was a perk, not a reason, but it was a nice perk, since she and her daughter had always been close.

She dialed her number and moved to the kitchen while the phone was ringing, sitting down at the big square bar in the middle and checking behind her to make sure that there wasn't anything that was so run down that it would scare Emma. Emma was the kind of daughter who would quit her job and come immediately if she thought her mother actually needed her.

Shannon would have to be a little more careful with her. There wasn't too much chance that Alex was going to do something so drastic, but Emma had been a little bit more protective of her and held a lot more hard feelings toward their father.

"Hello?" Emma's voice, familiar and beloved, came over the phone as her face came into view.

"Did I catch you while you were eating?" Shannon said immediately, not wanting to bother her.

"No. We're done." She grinned and then flipped the phone around. "This is my coworker, Brian."

"Hi, Brian," Shannon said. She felt a little queasy. She wasn't sure she was ready for her daughter to have a serious boyfriend.

"Hi, Ms. McKay." Brian grinned, showcasing a dimple at the corner of his mouth. He was handsome and looked successful and serious, and yet he had a twinkle of humor in his eye. A perfect man for Emma, and Shannon's heart squeezed.

"So, Mom, you made it okay?" Emma said, getting off her chair and walking through her apartment.

"I can talk to you later. I don't want to interrupt you and Brian."

"It's not a big deal. I'm actually at his place, and he's going to clean up since I cooked. I've got a few minutes."

There was her daughter, living her life, eating supper at a man's apartment. Wow. She'd thought four years of college would have gotten her ready for the idea that her daughter was going to have a life completely separate from her, but it was still taking a little bit to get used to.

"He seems like a really nice guy. I could see the twinkle in his eye, and I'm guessing he has a pretty good sense of humor."

"He does, and he's so smart, too," Emma said, her voice lowering, as though she didn't want Brian to hear what she was saying. "He's a Christian as well. I met him at church, and then we realized we work together. Mom, he's everything I've ever wanted."

"Just don't take it too fast," Shannon said, even though her daughter hadn't asked for her input.

"I know, Mom. He feels the same way. We're just eating. We're gonna chat a little, maybe watch a movie, but I'm going home."

"Good to know."

"What about you? Did you make it to Raspberry Ridge?"

"I did."

"Looks like you're sitting in the kitchen. Did you rent a cottage or something?"

"Not exactly." She took a breath. She wasn't trying to hide anything from her children. She didn't want them to hide anything from her. And Emma had always been an open book. Even now, she didn't have to tell her mother what she was doing tonight, but she had, because she knew it would ease her mind. "I bought an inn. This is the kitchen."

"You bought an inn?"

"Yes. It needs a little bit of fixing up, but... I'm feeling really excited about it."

"Okay," Emma said, and she seemed thoughtful. "Mom, you seem kind of sad."

Emma could always read between the lines and see more than she should have been able to.

"I suppose that's natural after a person's gone through what I've gone through," she said, and her voice was gentle.

She didn't want to bad-mouth her husband, but a person didn't have the last almost thirty years of their life blow up in their face and get over it easily.

"But you do seem kind of...maybe not excited, but hopeful. I am worried about you though. An inn?"

"It's going to be a grand adventure. I haven't gotten to have very many of those. I mean, of course we've gone on vacations, but it's always been me doing whatever your dad wanted to do. And now... I guess I get to live—" She stopped abruptly. She didn't want to live for herself. That seemed selfish and shallow. "Not for myself, because I envision this to be a place where people can come and heal, or be happy, or make memories as a family together. You know how much of a blessing our vacations were and how we always wanted to go back to every place we were at, just because we loved it so much and had such great memories there. We cherish our vacation pictures."

"You're right. I was just thinking about that time we went to New England, and Dad got lost, and there was no phone service and we didn't have any maps in the car, and I'm pretty sure we drove in a big honking circle up one mountain and down another and then up that mountain and back down another and... I think we spent the entire day lost." She laughed. "But we found the best overlooks. We couldn't even find them again because we couldn't figure out where we were to begin with. But I think that was one of my favorite vacations, and it was totally unplanned."

"I was scared to death we were going to run out of gas, and we hadn't passed a gas station the entire day because I think you're right, we kept going in a circle and there were no gas stations in that circle."

"I never even knew you were worried. We were just having the time of our lives. The windows were rolled down, we had our hands out there, we passed very few other cars, and if I recall correctly, some of the roads were even dirt."

"Yeah. Looking back, it's a lot of fun, but I was scared to death." She laughed. "But you're right, the views were amazing. We saw so many things that we would never have seen if we had had a map or phone service or if we hadn't taken a wrong turn somewhere."

"Yeah. I don't know that Dad really enjoyed it, but he kind of joined in with us and pretended that everything was okay."

"That's what parents do sometimes," Shannon said with a grin.

"Is that what you're doing now?" Emma asked, and the question was unexpected. And Shannon felt her smile slipping a bit before she propped it up deliberately.

"No. It's not. I'm excited about my future and about this inn. And it might not work out. It might be a total bust, but I'm going to have fun while I'm doing it. I wish I would have enjoyed that day on vacation so long ago instead of worrying the entire time about gas." She lifted her shoulder. "Everything worked out in the end."

Maybe she was pretending a little bit for her daughter. But she definitely didn't want Emma to worry about her.

"I'd like to come see you. Some weekend soon?" Emma said, and Shannon didn't have to fake her smile.

"I'd love that," she said, and she didn't have to fake any happiness about it.

They chatted a bit more before hanging up.

Shannon sat at the bar, looking at her phone, thoughts and feelings swirling through her. She was alone, by herself, her children were both happy and successful and living their own lives. She didn't know what she was going to do. She had this huge project in front of her, and while she hadn't lied to either one of her children, and she truly was excited about the challenge, she was also scared to death.

She didn't want to sit and ruminate on it. There was plenty of time for her to take a walk before it got dark, so she grabbed her jacket and then walked out the door, going down the hill to the path along the bluffs. She and Lance had actually spent a lot of time on that path, and it was worn smooth by decades of couples and dreamers, walking along, enjoying the lake view, maybe dreaming the way she was now. Or avoiding their thoughts, similar to her as well.

She and Lance had spent an entire year meeting out here and watching the sunset. She stood, her hands in the pockets of her coat as the sky changed colors and the sun sank slowly. The lake rippling and reflecting the sunlight back.

So many memories wrapped up in this view.

She and Lance had talked about their hopes and their dreams, their plans for college and beyond. In fact, she had forgotten about it until now, but this was the exact spot where Lance had shyly offered her a promise ring. It wasn't an engagement ring, and he wasn't asking her to marry him, but he wanted her to know that he was sincere, and while she had dreams of college and beyond, and he did too, he wanted her to know that she was the only one he would ever want. She remembered him saying something along those lines.

Had he been serious? Had he really not gotten married to anyone in the time that she'd been gone? She knew he hadn't been married before she left. In fact, his sister had been in a car accident while she and James had been away at college and then law school. And she had heard that Lance had stayed to help with her care.

She wondered about that now. At the time, someone had said that his sister would recover physically, but mentally she would always have issues, but she didn't remember what they were. And honestly, she'd been wrapped up in herself, in her own family, since she and James had had a child unexpectedly while James still had several years of law school left. She had her hands full juggling work and childcare and trying to support him, and she ended up dropping out of college.

That was why Yolanda was so much older than the other children.

She couldn't remember exactly what had been going on with Lance's sister, who was a good bit younger than he was.

As she was racking her brain, footsteps interrupted her reverie.

She looked up to see Lance approaching in running gear. Obviously, this was his normal jogging route.

He saw her about the same time she saw him, and she could see the surprise on his face, followed by what looked like pleasure, perhaps.

He slowed as he came to her and then stopped beside her, breathing hard but not panting.

"Beautiful evening," he said simply, his eyes lifting to the sunset which had exploded across the sky in a riot of colors.

"It's pretty," she said, knowing her words were inadequate for the display of immense beauty that swept across the sky. She'd forgotten how glorious the sunsets could be over the lake.

They stood in silence for a while as his breathing slowed, and she felt comfortable. Interestingly. Although that long-ago memory, the promise ring, the idea that she had taken that ring, and made a promise, and then broken it barely a month into her first semester of college, bothered her.

Was she any better than James? A promise ring was a promise. Of course, she and Lance had had a relationship, but it wasn't a marriage.

She hadn't made vows to him, just made a promise.

But she felt guilty for breaking it even more so than she had back then. The conversation that they had when she called him to tell him that she'd found someone else had been hard and awkward, and she was pretty sure Lance was crying when he got off the phone. She'd felt bad about it for a while. And then, all through her marriage, she knew for a certainty that she'd made the wrong decision, but once the vows had been said, there wasn't anything she could do to change it, other than what her husband had done, which was to go back on her promises and break vows that had been made before God.

She didn't know how long they had been standing there, but it had been a while. Lance hadn't said anything else, and she hadn't felt the need to either. It was a comfortable silence. Maybe the kind of silence that friends who had been friends and had known each other, everything about each other, years ago, could have.

"Are you really gonna stay this time?" Lance finally asked, breaking the silence with a casual question that probed deeply.

She found herself being able to be more honest with Lance than she could with either one of her children and maybe even with herself.

"I don't know if I'm brave enough."

Five

S hannon stood in front of the church, looking up at the large, white building. The views of the lake were magnificent even from the parking lot—she could only imagine what it would look like inside.

That morning, she'd woken up with an inexplicable urge to attend church. She'd done so regularly as a child and as a new, married wife, even when her husband had been too busy. Finally, with his job as a lawyer, she no longer even asked if he wanted to go. She'd gone by herself for years with the kids, and then somehow when Emma left for college, she quit. It hadn't been something she'd deliberately chosen to do, she just hadn't gotten up to go anymore. But this morning, she felt a longing like she hadn't had in years to step inside the familiar walls, sing the familiar hymns, feel the peace and serenity that always washed over her when she stepped into the Lord's house.

She also longed to be challenged from God's word. She had been a regular Bible reader for years, but that had fallen by the wayside too.

Perhaps her husband's betrayal and the divorce wouldn't have been quite so hard if she had been closer to the Lord through it all.

Still, she stood at the entrance, feeling a little insecure. Going to church was something she had always loved to do, but stepping foot into a new church, or at least one that she hadn't been to in almost two decades, was intimidating.

She noticed a couple getting out of their car, and she stepped aside, as though staring at the lake, admiring the view. Like that was the reason she hadn't walked into the building.

To her amazement, instead of walking around her, the couple walked right up to her and stopped.

"Hello, I'm Homer Aiken, this is my wife, Skyler. I don't think we've seen you around here lately?" His tone was polite, his words gentle.

Shannon immediately felt at ease.

She put her hand in his and shook it, and then shook Skyler's hand. "I'm back after a long time. I think I remember you, Homer. You live right next to the healing garden now. There used to be a gazebo there, and brambles and scrub brush, when I was growing up."

"I think the gazebo might have been before my time," Homer said, and there was a smile on his face and humor in his voice, which brought a smile to Shannon's face as well.

"Probably. I do think you're closer to my children's age, although slightly older than they are."

"I vaguely remember. You had two girls and a boy. And then... There was that tragedy." His voice trailed off, and Shannon nodded.

"That's correct. We moved away right after that, and I haven't been back. But I woke up this morning with a longing to go to church. It's just..." She let her voice trail off, unable to put into words how intimidating it was to walk into a new church not knowing anyone very well.

Skyler seemed to understand immediately. "Church can be so overwhelming. Everyone knows everyone else, and it's like a big family. That can feel a little exclusive to someone who is stepping in for the first time in a long time. I'd love it if you'd sit with us."

Shannon looked down at the little girl who held Skyler's hand and then at the baby in Homer's arms. Such a sweet family. Full of hopes and dreams the way she had been with her little ones. Although, most of the time her husband hadn't been with her. She appreciated their hopeful expressions and felt like maybe she would be intruding since her family had blown up so badly. But they didn't know that. Not yet anyway, although it was a small town and soon they would.

Still, she appreciated Skyler reaching out and extending the invitation to make her feel welcome.

"I'd love it if that would be okay."

"As long as you don't mind that the little ones are going to be with us. Usually there's a nursery, but there's a special speaker today, and in order that everyone can hear, they've canceled the nursery and junior church."

"Oh, I don't mind at all," she said, looking down into the big blue eyes of the little girl beside her.

"This is Saylor," Skyler said, pulling her hand away from where Homer had held it and slipping it into the crook of Shannon's elbow. "Trust me, when I first came here, I knew no one, and it was very intimidating. At least you've lived here at one time. And kind of know what to expect."

"You were from a big city?" Shannon asked as Skyler gently led her into the building.

"Yes, Chicago. It was definitely an adjustment coming here. Intimidating, too, since I didn't know anyone. But people were wonderful and so welcoming. That was a few years ago, and things haven't changed. In fact, if anything, we've had a rash of second chances here lately. Perhaps you're next."

"Perhaps," Shannon said, but inside she was laughing hysterically. There wasn't a chance that she was next. She was just running. Running from her life and coming here. Although... It felt like coming home. She really didn't know what she wanted, what she felt. She just knew she needed to be in church.

Skyler guided her to a seat and sat down beside her with Saylor on her lap.

Saylor seemed to be charmed by Shannon, who had always been rather good with children if she did say so herself. She'd volunteered in the church nursery and taught the preschool class at Bible school and for Sunday school for years. But as her children grew and she had more responsibilities during their high school years, she handed those responsibilities in the church over to other people, which made it easier for her to leave, since no one was going to miss her and she didn't have to find anyone to cover for her.

Maybe it was good to stay involved. It kept a person accountable.

Regardless, she stood, singing the familiar hymns, barely needing the hymnbook. When one had grown up singing all the verses of hymns all her life, a person had a tendency to memorize, and Shannon was gratified to note that the hymns came easily to her lips. She loved that they sang them with the piano and hadn't gone the way of a lot of larger, big-city churches where there was a band on the stage and songs that she didn't know coming from the speakers.

Maybe that was another reason she'd felt pushed out of church. It hadn't been anything that was familiar to her, and she'd missed the edifying words and beautiful melodies of the old hymns, knowing that they had withstood generations of testing and encouraged millions everywhere.

Regardless, she pulled her Bible out and opened to the passage. The pastor had them stand while he read.

The passage and message was on the prodigal son, but instead of focusing on the son, the pastor focused on the father. He talked about the father's love for the son, no matter what the son was doing. And spoke on how God didn't love us because we were worthy, but it was His love that made us worthy.

It was something that Shannon hadn't thought about for a really long time. God loved her. He loved her, no matter what happened and no matter whether her husband did or not. Having her husband toss her away like so much trash had made her feel...less than. She hadn't even realized it until just then, as tears pricked her eyes. She felt like garbage. But it wasn't James who should or could make her feel worthy. It was God. It was what God thought that mattered. Not James.

A soft hand touched her cheek, startling her out of her thoughts, and she glanced down to see Saylor putting her hand on her cheek.

She smiled softly at the girl, who climbed from where she had been sitting and coloring with her crayons in the pew to Shannon's lap. Skyler glanced over, apologizing, but Shannon smiled and shook her head, indicating that it was just fine.

By then, Saylor had taken both of Shannon's cheeks in her chubby little hands and was staring into her eyes, almost as though she had never seen a face before.

The little girl was sweet, and after a few seconds, she turned and snuggled into Shannon's arms.

The innocent acceptance, along with the timely reminder that God loved her, cracked something in Shannon's heart. Or maybe it healed a little bit of something.

Whatever it was, Shannon was very glad that she had accepted the invitation to sit with them and that she had gone to church in the first place.

After the service, there was coffee and apple cider donuts being served. Shannon thought she probably knew where the apple cider donuts came from. She limited herself to just one, and it was just as amazing as it had been when she had eaten it in Lauren's store.

She had a donut in one hand and a coffee in the other when she came face-to-face with Pastor Garnett and his wife.

"Welcome to Raspberry Ridge," Pastor Garnett said. He laughed at her full hands. "Fellowship is an awkward time for introductions," he said with a chuckle.

"But we're happy to meet you anyway," the woman beside him said. "I'm the pastor's wife, Mertie, and we're happy to have you here."

"It's good to be here. Even though it was maybe a little bit difficult to come. Your message was exactly what I needed."

Pastor Garnett nodded his head. "God often meets us where we are. It's funny how that works."

"I promise you he doesn't know any of your story, but it is funny how a lot of times messages just speak into our soul and give us what we need. I certainly needed messages of redemption to remind me that nothing that I did was beyond something God could forgive."

Shannon blinked. "You used to be a Christian speaker, didn't you?" Something about what Mertie had said resonated in her soul. She seemed to recall that Mertie had had a child but had given it up for adoption because it didn't fit in with her Christian speaker lifestyle. But then, she kind of disappeared from public view after saying she was going back to her family and piecing it all together.

From what Shannon could remember, Pastor Garnett was not the father of the child, but she couldn't remember for sure. But obviously they were happy together now. And it was good to know that a person's past didn't have to define their future, that God could forgive anything, that He could take the broken pieces and build a beautiful family.

"I was. I'm not anymore. I realized that family was far more important and helping just a few people deeply and completely was better for me than being a blessing to millions, especially if that meant my family got the short end of the stick." She lifted her shoulder. "Maybe that's not everyone's best choice, but it was definitely mine."

"And we've all benefited from it," Pastor Garnett said, putting his arm around his wife and drawing her close.

They shared such a tender and sweet look that Shannon felt the sudden urge to cry. She had wanted a love like that. A love where her husband drew her near and looked down on her like she was the only woman in the world, and wanted her beside him, and gave her the credit that she deserved for keeping the family together and for doing everything in her power to make his life more comfortable and peaceful.

She supposed she would never get any credit for that. But she had to remind herself that life wasn't about the credit that she got. That God was watching, and that anything she deserved—any kind of reward she deserved—would eventually be given to her by Him. She just had to continue to try to live her life while trying to be more like Jesus.

"You must be Shannon McKay." A woman's voice interrupted her thoughts. A tall lady, distinguished looking but with a friendly smile, walked up with her hand out.

"I am," Shannon said, grasping her hand.

"I'm Vera Miller. Dominic's wife. He was out to give you an estimate for your inn."

"He was." Shannon smiled. "He said that you specialized in healing designs and that I might be interested in some of your services as well."

"He had mentioned the same to me. I guess one of the things I wanted to say when I saw you was that I am happy to offer my services for free. Anyone who is brave enough to take on the inn needs as much help as she can get."

Somehow her smile made her feel like a friend immediately, and

Shannon found herself smiling back. "I'll definitely take all the help I can get," she said. "But I can't let you work for free."

"I insist. Honestly, Dominic and I have more than what we can use for ourselves and even for our children. It would be really nice to be able to give back something that would benefit the community and anyone who came to our town. Don't feel like you have to accept my offer, but it's there." She smiled, her eyes going to several children who were bouncing around the man Shannon recognized as Dominic. "Before my kids claim me again, I also wanted to extend an invitation to our women's Bible study. We're reading about second chances." Her smile was gentle. "It seems like it might be fitting."

"Very much so," Shannon said, realizing that Vera had seen straight through her somehow. Interestingly, it didn't make her feel defensive. Although she didn't feel like sharing much either. She just felt seen.

Vera told her the day and time, and Shannon said that she would try as hard as she could to be there.

They were chatting about the inn and about some of the things that Dominic had told Vera, when movement by the door caught Shannon's eye.

Lance walked in. And her heart stopped.

She hadn't said anything more to him on the bluffs after she admitted that she didn't know whether she was brave enough to stay. She had made some kind of excuse and hurried away back to the inn, and he hadn't tried to stop her nor follow her. Which, of course, she hadn't expected him to.

"Where have you been, Lance?" Pastor Garnett said as he held his hand out to shake Lance's.

Lance was not dressed in church clothes—in fact, it looked like he had been working.

Shannon was close enough to hear everything as Lance said, "Mrs. James had a toilet that overflowed this morning when I went to pick her up to bring her to church. She needed my help to fix it, and one thing led to another, and I ended up opening up the shop and buying an entirely new toilet. Somehow hers had cracked overnight, which seems odd, but she claims she has no idea how it could have happened."

"Wow. That sounds like a mess," Pastor Garnett said. "I really appreciate you helping some of our elderly church members get here on time, but I didn't realize that you were going to need to use your skills as well."

They laughed together, and that's when Lance glanced around and caught her eye.

He smiled, not pushing, not even questioning. Just accepting that she was there and looking like he was glad of it.

And she was glad he was. She thought of all the times that her husband hadn't bothered to go with her to church, and the idea that Lance not only went but helped other people get there, and that he still came, even though he was too late to actually be at the service, spoke to her heart.

Definitely coming to church this morning had been an excellent idea. She felt, not like she could handle anything that life threw at her, but like maybe the town was just what she needed, and she had been reminded that God loved her, which was something else she had desperately longed for. Without even knowing it.

Six

The next day, Monday morning, Dominic's crew arrived, and there was major chaos as he sent different groups to work in different areas.

After Vera had spoken with Shannon at church, Dominic had come over and said basically the same thing that she had—anyone who was brave enough to renovate the inn and provide a place for people to stay in Raspberry Ridge was someone that they wanted to help as much as they could. He had mentioned a figure that was so low that Shannon couldn't keep from gasping in surprise, and then she agreed immediately.

She was pretty sure that what he was going to charge her wasn't even going to cover the cost of his workers, but she remembered what Vera had said about Dominic and her having more than what they needed and wanting to be able to help the community. Apparently they thought helping her was helping the community that she was in. And really it was. When she opened the inn, it would be a blessing to everyone. That was her hope, anyway.

Regardless, Shannon buckled the new tool belt that she had bought at the hardware store around her waist and waited for Dominic to get done giving orders to all of his crew before she approached him.

"What can I do?" she asked.

He looked at her in surprise, his eyes going to her tool belt before back up and meeting her gaze. "I wasn't expecting—"

"I'm here, and I want a job. Or I guess I could kind of go off on my own and see what I can get into."

Dominic laughed. "I promise you, we can take care of it."

"I want to." She said it with firmness, and his eyes flicked back to hers, drilling in and seeming to understand that it wasn't that she wanted to—she needed to.

"All right. By now, the first crew I sent out should be almost done putting drywall up in the closet of the first room off the lobby. That's a new crew, and the best place to learn is a closet. You can do the spackling."

She couldn't help but feel relief. A closet was an excellent spot to learn—Dominic was absolutely right. If she screwed up, it wouldn't be nearly as obvious.

"I'll do it until I learn it."

"All right. I'll be in in a little bit to give you a few pointers, but for now, I need to go and make sure that everybody is doing what they're supposed to be doing. I'm not worried about you doing your best." He smiled at her, a gentle smile that made her feel understood.

He walked away, and Shannon turned toward the room he had spoken of.

Sure enough, when she got there, the crew had already finished in the closet and had picked up their tools and headed out.

Shannon had to admit she was relieved to be by herself. Learning a new task was not usually something that one appreciated having an audience for.

She pulled out her phone and looked up some videos in order to get herself familiar with what she would be doing.

She thought she had the basics and decided that she would start at the top and work down. Probably the easier part would be the bottom, and she believed in doing the hardest first.

Pulling a small stepladder over, she stepped up on the first step. She had to blame it on the tool belt, whose weight she was not used to. It pulled her to the side a little, and she ended up losing her balance and falling into the wall. Somehow, her elbow and shoulder managed to make a big hole in the drywall.

Seriously? she thought to herself as she pulled herself out of the wall.

She wasn't hurt at all, and she was again glad that there had been no witnesses.

"Are you okay?" a deep voice said, and she retracted the idea of no witnesses immediately.

She recognized that voice too. It sent a shiver down her spine. The very best kind. Except it wasn't a good time—it was never a good time to be caught doing something embarrassing, like losing one's balance on a stepladder and creating more work for themselves.

"I'm fine. Just my pride is injured."

"Well, that's easily fixed. There wasn't anyone around to see you anyway, except for me, and I've done the very same thing multiple times. And I would guess I've had more experience in drywalling than you when I did it as well."

"If you've done any drywall at all, you have more experience than me."

"All right. Then yes. I have more experience than you. I've fallen into drywall and punched holes in it with not just my body but with a hammer, accidentally—I wasn't angry or anything." Lance grinned at her, and she couldn't help but grin back. "I've done it with a bucket. Don't ask me how I did that one, because I'm still not sure. And also with my ladder, where I did lose my balance and fall off the ladder, and I kept myself from falling into the drywall, but my ladder tilted and fell into the wall and created a hole. So there, I've got you beat."

"Well, good to know. You definitely have made me feel better about my clumsiness."

"I wouldn't say it's clumsiness. Just a lack of proficiency in doing something that you are just learning to do."

He made her feel better. Truly. Like it wasn't really dumb to put a hole in the wall. Even though she knew it was, and she half wondered if maybe he was exaggerating how many times he had put holes in himself. But he explained every time to her, and it sounded legit. Plus, Lance was not a liar.

"What are you doing here?" she asked, for lack of anything better to say. She needed to get her phone up and figure out how to fix the hole. Because she was pretty sure she couldn't just put spackling over it. But she didn't want to do that in front of Lance, and for some reason, she didn't want to ask for his help either. Maybe it was pride.

"I subcontract to Dominic at times, and when he told me that he was going to be working on the inn, I jumped at the chance. I have Tyler helping me at the store, running the register and taking care of customers. We're usually not super busy on Mondays."

"Oh. I didn't realize you had help."

"It's more profitable for me to work for Dominic. Although, I understand that this is a worthy cause, and we're donating our time."

"I offered to pay," she said, feeling like she wanted to make sure that he knew that she wasn't trying to take advantage of anyone. She really wasn't.

"I know," he said, putting his hand up as though to ward off any other protestations she might make. "And I agree that it was a worthy cause. Plus, I happen to like the owner. A lot."

She could feel her cheeks heating, and she turned back toward the wall. "I have no idea how to fix this." There. It wasn't so hard to admit when she was trying to deflect, or maybe run away from, the feelings that Lance seemed to be sharing.

She didn't want that. She didn't want anything. She just wanted to... be left alone, but not be left alone. If that made sense.

"Well, it's a good thing I know. And I can show you how." He paused, as though a little afraid of his next words. "That is, if you don't mind."

"No. Of course not. I want to learn. I need to help with this. I can't just have everyone else doing everything while I sit around."

"Well, it wouldn't hurt for someone to make some food. If we're going to be here as much as I think we're going to be, it probably would be nice for there to be a regular meal. Just one."

"That's a really good idea. I'll have to think about that. I think I can do both, because I definitely don't want to not work just so I can cook. And even if I do cook, I'm still going to need to work."

"I'm sure you can do both. Even if you cook in the morning and work in the afternoon."

She nodded, somehow not wanting to remove herself from the work but also loving the idea of providing everyone who was helping with the inn with a hot meal. It was too late for today, because she would have to make a grocery list and go pick things up—she definitely didn't have enough stuff in her pantry to cook for this many people.

"I wonder if Dominic knows exactly how many people are here," she said as Lance moved around, picking a few things up and moving closer to her.

"I'm sure he does. You could probably have him text you every morning with how many people are going to be arriving, if that would be something that would be helpful. And not too late." He paused, and then he held up what looked to be tape, only it had holes in it. "This is what we use to fix this hole. Let me show you how."

It was funny how easily they settled into a rhythm. How comfortable she felt with him, how patient he was with her, and how at ease she was. They worked together with an ease that she didn't feel with too many people. Several people commented on it as they came and went during the day. Even while Shannon had in the back of her mind the idea that she would be cooking for everyone tomorrow, she would miss working with Lance, because she wasn't sure she'd ever worked with someone that well before. And considering that she'd never done drywall before, that was saying something.

"Excuse me," a man's voice said from the entrance to the room where they were now working. They'd spackled the entire closet, and Lance had explained that it was going to need to dry before they could wipe it down and sand it and put another coat of spackling on where it was needed. "I'm looking for Shannon."

"I'm Shannon," she said in answer to the man's statement.

"I'm Trevor. Trevor Gillette, and I heard that you might be in need of some custom woodworking. I wanted to come and offer my services."

"Oh my goodness. Custom woodworking? That sounds fancy." And expensive.

"It's my love. And with everyone else in town talking with so much excitement about the inn opening, I was hoping that I might be able to offer my services, for free, just so I can have a little bit of a hand in it. You wouldn't believe the wildfire that you've started with the idea that you're going to fix this old place up. And that there might actually be paying customers coming here. And a place for us to go too."

"I hope so. That's the dream anyway."

"It's a good dream," Trevor said, coming over and shaking hands with Lance. They appeared to know each other, so Shannon didn't bother with introductions, considering that she had just met Trevor.

"I don't even know where to start," Shannon said, looking around.

"Dominic told me to check with you, but he said that he could use banisters and molding around the tops and bottoms of the rooms, particularly in the entryway. Also, the porch needs to be redone. My buddy Josiah is pretty handy as well and in fact better at that kind of thing than I am. He couldn't be here today, because he's working on a yacht, but he said to sign him up for whatever, and he'd be here. He said he would provide his own materials as well."

Shannon was overwhelmed. People were going to provide their own materials? They were going to do this for free? She could barely fathom the idea of a town coming together like this. But it must have been like Trevor had said, and people were really excited about the inn opening.

"Yes to anything that you want to do," Shannon finally said. "Although, some of these things just look so terrible that I don't know that there's really much of anything that we can do to make it look better."

Trevor grinned. "That's pretty much my job. To find the beauty underneath something that doesn't look like much of anything. Even things that look like they're ruined have beauty inside. It just takes the right hands to bring it out."

Shannon blinked at him. He could be talking about her. About...the right hands. She wasn't sure who the right hands would be. Maybe God, just moving in her life.

"Shannon and I have been working in that room all day. We'll be there tomorrow, so if you have any questions, just pop in, and we'll answer as best we can." Lance shook Trevor's hand again, and Trevor walked away.

Or it could be Lance. Working with him today had felt like coming home in a way that even coming back to Raspberry Ridge hadn't felt like. It brought back all of the things that they had done in high school together. So much time, so many dreams shared, and so much compatibility. She realized just exactly how much she and James did not jive. If that was a good word for it.

James just was himself, and she was there to serve him, which she didn't mind. That was the kind of person she was, always looking for someone to help. She was happy to be able to help her husband, help him to have a law career and to climb and be successful in whatever he wanted to do. The same with her children. That was what she wanted. She wanted to be a blessing to people. But there was a certain satisfaction in having an equal partnership, which was what it felt like when she and Lance were working together, even though Lance was the one who had all the experience.

She was deep in thought as she climbed the ladder, so deep in thought that she wasn't paying attention and missed the second step. She slipped off and might have had another drywall catastrophe, except Lance was there to catch her, steady her, and hold her until she caught her balance.

It took her a second to realize that she was clutching his shoulders, their bodies pressed together, his eyes looking down on her with an expression on his face that she couldn't quite read. She didn't know about him, but her heart beat erratically, and she felt a heat that was unfamiliar but not unpleasant.

She jerked away immediately and swallowed, her mouth suddenly dry. "I better go check the pantry, if I'm going to make it to the grocery store before it closes tonight. Thanks for your help."

She hurried out of the room. Knowing that once again, she was running.

Seven

That evening, Shannon sat at the table, struggling to figure out a menu. She didn't know why it was so hard. Maybe because she'd spent most of her time castigating herself for running away from Lance. It had been almost quitting time anyway, but the guys had been gone for more than an hour, and she still hadn't come up with meals and an ingredient list.

What could she make that would serve everyone and would still allow her to have time to work?

She had a crockpot, but one crockpot wasn't going to be enough. Dominic had told her that usually there would be around ten to twelve men there every day—that included Trevor and Josiah.

She still hadn't figured it out when there was a knock at the front door.

Who in the world would be here now?

It was only six o'clock and still a little bit light out, but even so, a tiny shiver went down Shannon's spine. She was here by herself, and the town was a ten-minute walk away.

It was only a couple of minutes by car, but still. She was pretty far off the beaten path. Like she had thought the night she got there, it was a great place to hide out, but it was also a great place to...commit a crime? Is that what she was thinking? That someone was here to commit a crime?

She tried to reason with herself. Someone who was here to commit a crime would not be knocking on the front door.

With that thought bolstering her courage, she marched to the door and almost yanked it open.

Standing in front of her was a well-dressed woman, but she had the weary look of someone who was running from something.

"Hello," Shannon said.

"Hi, my name is Marina Castellano." The woman's voice was cultured. "I'm recently relocated from up north. I have extensive fine dining experience, and I understood from overhearing a conversation in town that you might be looking for a chef." She gave a nervous smile. "I believe I can handle all of the demands that might occur, including breakfast, lunch, and dinner, no matter how fancy or plain you might like it to be."

That was quite an introduction, and Shannon couldn't believe God's providence. Really? She was struggling with a menu, and Marina knocks on the door and offers her chef services?

That seemed a little too good to believe, but sometimes God worked that way. And here He was, orchestrating everything now so that people were inspired to donate their time, and she wasn't dipping into her stash of money quite as much as what she'd feared she would.

"Well, I...don't know what to say."

"I don't think there's much to say. I could cook for you right now if you'd like, using whatever ingredients you have in the cupboard, and you can see for yourself whether you think I will be any good for you or not."

"I'm not sure I'll be able to pay you." She could probably pay her something, since she wasn't spending as much on everything else, but a chef was a wish list item, a fantasy item, something that she didn't actually need, and she didn't want to spend money on that until she knew for sure she wasn't going to have to spend it somewhere else.

"I can start immediately, and I'll just work for room and board. We can continue with that arrangement until you're ready to discuss salary."

If it were up to Shannon, she might think that the woman was being a little bit evasive. Although her confidence was almost overshadowing everything else. But why else would she be willing to work for room and board?

Shannon recalled the old saying of not looking a gift horse in the mouth. Perhaps she should not question too far. The woman was obviously well-dressed and well-spoken. She came from some type of upper class, Shannon would bet, whether it was just working for them or belonging to them, Shannon wasn't sure. Not that it mattered. It was her cooking skills that really mattered, and Shannon thought her offer of making a meal on the spot was a pretty good one, considering there was a very limited amount of groceries in the pantry.

"All right, I'll take you up on that. Come on in."

Maybe it was her imagination, but Marina seemed relieved, excessively so.

She was pretty sure she didn't imagine the fact that Marina looked over her shoulder before the door closed behind her.

It was on the tip of her tongue to ask Marina if she was running from something, but she didn't. After all, Marina could ask her the same question, and if she were being honest, she would have to answer yes, she was running from more than one something.

She was running from her husband and the divorce and the life that had imploded back in Detroit, but she was also running from the feelings that she had felt for Lance today. She hadn't offered him any other explanation but had run out of the room, and he deserved better. He hadn't done anything wrong. He'd saved her from making a mess in the drywall again, and she hadn't even thanked him. Just run away. He must think she was the most horrible person ever. Although, she knew that wasn't the way Lance was, and he didn't think any such thing.

"This is the kitchen, and you are the one who offered, but I do have to warn you that there are not very many ingredients with which to work." She went over to the cupboard and opened it, showing the few items that she had bought recently. There was nothing else.

Looking at them, she had no idea what in the world Marina could possibly make out of them.

"Oh, and there's a little bit of milk and some eggs in the refrigerator here." She also had bought a little bit of cheese and a couple of fresh vegetables.

If Marina could make a meal out of that, she was hired on the spot. Not that Shannon would turn down anyone who was offering to work for room and board.

"Oh, that's not going to be a problem," Marina said with a smile.

And she got to work immediately. They chatted while Marina was working, although anytime the subject went to Marina's past, she was very evasive. Even her explanations of her work experience were general and not specific. She spoke about working in a restaurant, but she didn't mention where that restaurant was.

It made Shannon exceptionally curious, but she had to respect Marina's privacy—after all, she wanted her own privacy respected. By the time Marina set a bowl of delicious-looking pasta with fresh vegetables and sauce in front of her, Shannon was starving and practically drooling from the delicious smell.

"You'll have to let me know what you think," Marina said, but her expression indicated that she wasn't worried. Like she knew it was going to be good.

Shannon couldn't eat by herself. "Get a plate for yourself and sit down. I'll pray, and we can eat together."

Marina's brows lifted a bit in surprise, but she did as she was told without further comment. When her plate was ready, Shannon bowed her head and thanked the Lord for the food. In her heart, she thanked God for sending her the gift of Marina as well, and she also prayed for whatever it was that was causing Marina to have such a skittish feel to her. She prayed for wisdom that God would let her know when it was time to pry and time to step back and let Marina have her secrets.

As she suspected, her first bite was absolutely amazing, and she could barely wait to swallow before she said, "You're hired. You're hired, and I don't care how much you're charging me, you're hired."

"Room and board is all I ask."

They ate together, not saying much.

As they finished up, Shannon said, "I can do the dishes, if you'd like to sit and plan a menu for the week. We have ten to twelve men who work here every day, and I said I would provide something warm and nutritious for them to eat midday. You and I can probably eat leftovers every evening, if you just cook enough, or whatever. But we need a grocery list, and I need to go get something, because we obviously don't have enough to even provide a meal for tomorrow."

"No. It was stretching it a little bit to get the meal for this evening. I probably could do it if I had to, but I would prefer to have groceries on hand. And staples as well. I take it there's no flour or sugar?"

"No. And I don't want to have extravagant five-star restaurant meals, but we could provide lunch and dessert every day, as well as tea and water to drink."

Marina nodded her head and pulled her phone out of her purse.

As Shannon did the dishes, Marina worked on her phone.

Before Shannon was finished, her phone buzzed, and Shannon turned around in time to see a panicked expression cross Marina's face.

She glanced up and immediately tried to smooth it over. "I need to get this," she said softly. Then, she stood up from where she had been sitting at the bar and walked casually outside of the kitchen.

Perhaps she was trying to keep Shannon from hearing, but Shannon caught a little bit of the conversation. She didn't really mean to eavesdrop, but when she heard Marina say, "No. I told you I won't come back. Do not have me followed," she felt like she had to say something.

As Marina stepped back in, Shannon was finished, and she leaned against the counter, her hands in her pockets, trying to appear nonthreatening. She wanted to help Marina if she could.

"Is everything okay?" she asked, hoping Marina would confide in her.

"Sure. Everything's fine," Marina said, obviously trying to make it so that if she said it was fine, it was actually fine.

"I thought I heard you say something about being followed?"

Marina's eyes grew wide, and then she shook her head. "No. Not really. It's just... It's complicated. An ex, you know how they can be. But I'm fine here."

"All right. But if you need anything or you need me to help, I'm here." Shannon didn't know what else to say. She couldn't make Marina confide in her if she didn't want to. And it mirrored her own situation. Although she wasn't afraid for her life or afraid for anything, she was still running. Still trying to get away. And she had her own secrets. She felt very protective of Marina and her secrets.

"If you'll give me your number, I can text you the groceries that I'll need. If that's too much, I can try to pare it down." She waved a hand. "There's a lot of staples that we need to stock up on, and I wanted to make sure I got them all, plus things like ketchup and mustard and that type of thing."

"I get it. We're basically stocking a kitchen for the first time. It's bound to be a lot. Don't worry about it." She paused for a moment. "I was going to go this evening for the groceries. Would you like to come?"

Immediately Marina shook her head. "No thank you. I'll just stay here if that's okay."

"Of course. That's fine. Let me show you where you can stay. I thankfully have one more set of clean sheets and one room that is mostly put together. We might have to move you around a bit to completely finish it, but thankfully, it's livable." She had been tempted to use that room herself, and maybe she should have, because it wouldn't hurt for Marina to be sleeping close to the kitchen if she was going to be working in it. But for now, it would work.

She showed Marina the room, and Marina seemed grateful for her own space, thanking Shannon multiple times.

Shannon felt like she and Marina were going to be really good friends, but she wished there was something she could do to help the woman with the problem she obviously had.

"If you're okay, I'm going to leave."

"I'll be fine. I'll probably be in bed when you get back, because it's going to be an early morning. I assume you're going to want breakfast?"

"I didn't even think about that."

"It's okay. I just put ingredients for waffles and pancakes and eggs on the grocery list. Because I assumed you would want to eat a morning meal as well. Especially if you're going to be working all day."

"And you need to eat too," Shannon said.

Marina smiled gratefully and nodded.

Shannon thought about it as she drove into town, but she put it out of her mind as she drove through Raspberry Ridge.

Her eyes caught on the sign for the gym along Main Street. She couldn't imagine that the gym had many members in a town as small as Raspberry Ridge was. And then, on the spur of the moment, she stopped. She needed to stay in shape—after all, she couldn't help anyone if she were sick and didn't keep up with her own health. And since she had saved so much on the inn and the whole town was rallying around her, she could pass it on. She could buy a membership at the gym, and then after spending that kind of money, hopefully she would be inspired to make the trip a few times a week to work out.

She got out of her car, opened the door, and walked in. As she thought, the gym was almost deserted, with just two people on machines in the back.

Mateo, whom she had met at church, stood behind the counter. It was difficult to forget him, since he was so tall, with almost a military bearing.

He smiled when he saw her. "Shannon. Come on in."

"You remember my name," she said.

"Of course. Everyone's talking about you and the inn and how excited they are that it's going to be opening. You're the talk of the town."

"Oh my goodness. I feel like I might let people down if it doesn't work out."

"I'm sure people will be disappointed, but I wouldn't let that worry you." He seemed very casual and at ease. "Is there something I can help you with?"

"I want a membership. I think I'll pay for a year if that's okay." A year seemed good. Maybe she should pay for two. She should ground herself here as much as she could and not be tempted to run again. She needed to learn to stay and fight her battles, and Raspberry Ridge was the perfect place to take a stand.

"I'm happy to hear it. Not just for the business, but because it sounds like you're going to stay."

"Yes. I am." It wasn't as honest of an answer as she had given to Lance, but Mateo wasn't Lance. Lance was special.

"I'm glad to hear it. It's interesting the way the Lord sends exactly what we need. I was just sitting here trying to think how to drum up a little bit more business. I think maybe I need to figure out a plan to accommodate your inn guests."

"I'd be happy to put an advertisement up in the lobby so when we open, people know about your place. Maybe you could give them a special rate for a day or two or a week."

"Great idea. I'll get to work on that. I just love it when God sends what we need."

"Me too. Actually, God just sent me a chef this evening. I was wondering how I was going to cook and still work at the inn, and Marina showed up at my door."

"Marina? Italian? Dark hair, about this tall?" Mateo said. He described Marina to a T.

His interest was endearing.

"Yep. That's the one. Do you know her?"

"I met her on the street. She asked me where the inn was. She... seemed a little mysterious, like she was looking over her shoulder."

"Well, she's at the inn now, and anyone who wants her will have to go through me."

"I'm glad to hear that. Sometimes you meet someone and they just seem like they need someone to protect them." He didn't say that Marina was that person to him, but Shannon felt like she might have been.

It was sweet to see. And she was glad to know that Marina had two protectors now, though Mateo would be a much better protector than she was.

She finished signing up and then promised to come back with some workout clothes and be sure to utilize her membership.

She left feeling lighter in spirit and almost eager to see what else God had planned for her.

Eight

Tuesday evening, Shannon stood at Vera Miller's door. She'd already walked back to her car three times, and she knew if she didn't go in this time, she probably wouldn't.

She wasn't sure why she was so afraid, so reluctant to join. The warm lights spilled out from the windows, and laughter rang out quite often. She could even smell the faint scent of cinnamon buns. Marina had made a plate full of cookies that Shannon held in her hand. Marina had politely declined when Shannon had invited her to go along with her to the Bible study. Shannon wasn't sure whether it was because Marina was not a believer or whether it was because of whatever it was that Marina was afraid of and constantly seemed to be looking for over her shoulder.

The meal she had made for the men had been absolutely amazing, top notch, restaurant quality, and it had been well appreciated.

Shannon had enjoyed the meal a second time as leftovers before she had left for Bible study.

She felt bad for Marina, but unless Marina told her what the issue was, she really couldn't help her, other than letting her know that she was a supportive shoulder to lean on anytime she needed her.

She wished she had a supportive shoulder now. Lance would be welcome. She'd not managed to avoid working with him all day, but he had deliberately kept the conversation light, when they'd spoken at all. They worked so well together that conversation really wasn't needed. And by the time he left, she was sad to see him go and had almost forgotten her awkwardness around him.

Taking a deep breath, knowing that she was stalling, she lifted a hand and knocked on the door.

A voice called out, "Come in! It's unlocked!"

How nice. It was so friendly and welcoming that she didn't even need someone to answer the door for her. She could just walk in.

She had pushed the door open and stepped inside when Vera came hurrying out from the other room.

"I'm so glad you're here! I had just said to the group that I was hoping that you would come."

"I'm sorry I'm a little late," she said, lifting up the plate of cookies. "But I brought cookies."

"They look amazing," Vera said, taking the plate from her. "You know everyone here, but follow me and I'll introduce you. I know it's kind of hard to remember everyone's name when you first get to a new place."

Shannon appreciated the consideration. She had worked on names before she'd come, which had been part of her nervousness. She was just one person and easy to remember, but it was hard for her to remember who she'd been introduced to and who she hadn't.

She followed Vera into the living room where five or six ladies sat around the coffee table, which was filled with snacks from desserts to crackers to chips, and it seemed like everyone had a drink in front of them on a coaster. The living room itself wasn't fancy, but it was nice, with big windows and a cathedral ceiling, which made it feel spacious and welcoming.

"Please ignore all of the kid toys that are scattered around," Vera said over her shoulder.

Shannon hadn't even noticed them, but it was obvious that children lived in the home now that she glanced around.

"Be careful not to trip on anything, like I did," one of the ladies said. She was sitting on the floor, cross-legged, holding a drink in her hand,

and smiling. She looked friendly and young, and Vera introduced her as Grace.

One of Yolanda's friends. Shannon swallowed. She could handle this.

"It's great to see you again. You definitely look a lot different than the last time I saw you." She was a gangly teen at that age and at the time had been heartbroken over the loss of her friend.

"And smiling again," Grace said easily. "And a lot bigger." She laughed.

Vera introduced Mertie, whom Shannon remembered from church along with Skyler, and Olive. She also introduced Birdie, who was not a permanent resident of Raspberry Ridge but had a vacation home there.

"My work takes me away more than I like, but my husband and I come back as much as we can. This is our safe space," Birdie said with a friendly smile.

She had movie-star good looks, and Shannon bit her tongue rather than ask if she had ever starred in a movie. Surely the movie star that she was thinking about wasn't Birdie. But come to think of it, wasn't there a singer...?

It didn't matter. Birdie didn't mention it, and neither did anyone else, and maybe it was one of those things that, like Shannon, Birdie had things she'd rather not talk about. Shannon could respect that for sure.

"I understand you're back after a long time. That pretty much describes all of us." Olive, who hadn't said much, spoke from where she sat with her feet curled up underneath her on the recliner, a plate of snacks on her lap and a glass of what looked like milk in her hands.

"Yeah. I'm back after almost twenty years. I hope to stay."

"I hope you do too, especially since you're fixing up the inn. I'm looking forward to more business and tourists," Grace said.

Shannon nodded. "I think opening the inn will be good for everyone. The only thing is, I love the small-town atmosphere and the close-knit community. I hope that the inevitable expansion the inn will cause doesn't destroy the sense of community you guys have here. I felt welcome almost the second I set foot in town."

"That means we're doing our job," Mertie said. And everyone nodded.

Shannon had settled into one of the comfortable chairs after grabbing a few snacks from the table. She noticed that everyone took one of Marina's cookies, and she hoped they were as good as they smelled and looked.

After a little bit more chatter, Vera motioned to Mertie, and she began the meeting with a prayer.

She prayed like someone who knew God personally, which was the way Shannon always wanted to pray but didn't typically feel like she attained. It was no wonder that Mertie used to be a popular speaker. And she taught from the Bible like someone with a solid faith and lots of confidence that God was good and that she knew Him personally.

"When we look at the woman at the well, she was ashamed of what she had done and what she was in the middle of doing. But that didn't keep her from talking to Jesus."

"Sometimes it seems like we have to have a catastrophe first before we even start to talk to Jesus. At least that's the way it seems sometimes," Birdie said. She lifted a shoulder. "That's the way it was with me. Every time in my life I've had a major catastrophe, it's brought me closer to the Lord."

"And I think that's what those hard times in our lives are designed to do. To deepen our relationship with the Lord, to smooth off our rough edges and make us more like Jesus. But that's only if we let them," Mertie said while the other ladies nodded.

"When I hid my pregnancy and then tried to be a speaker, it just didn't feel right. I was successful, but it didn't make me a better person. It didn't make me better until I faced it, until I did what I knew I was supposed to do. That's when I grew."

"It was the same for me. My divorce was the absolute worst thing that ever happened to me, or so I thought. But it turned out to be the best," Grace said, and it hurt Shannon's heart to know that someone who had been so close to Yolanda had gone through a divorce as well. And at such a younger age. At least Shannon had thirty years of good memories with her family, and her kids were grown. It would have been terrible if her husband had decided to do everything that he had done when the kids were still at home and she would have had to deal with all of that as well.

The ladies were talking, discussing Grace's divorce and the benefits that had come out of it, and listening as Birdie shared about her trials as well.

Everyone had something to say, except for Shannon, who had been quiet.

Finally, there was a soft pause, and Mertie looked at Shannon. "I know you're new, but please don't be afraid to speak up if you'd like to share something. Sometimes it helps to talk things through. I think most of us have already processed a lot of the pain that we've been through," she huffed out a breath, "although I don't know that you ever completely recover from it. You can definitely see the good, see where God has worked, but hard times leave scars. They just do." She smiled again, softly and easily. "So, if you'd like to share, you're welcome, I think we all understand, but don't feel pressured."

"Well, I guess like several of you, I have a divorce. I'm still reeling from it, and I suppose it's hard. I definitely made some mistakes in my youth, and I can see almost a direct line from those mistakes to my divorce. But yeah, I'm trying to come out from the other side. I don't know if I'm at the point where I would say that it's the best thing that ever happened to me, but I can see good things coming out of it. I... I know my husband did his best, but I could have had a better man."

Maybe she shouldn't have added that last part. She didn't want to bad-mouth her husband. No one else had said anything unkind about anyone as they talked about their pain and grief. But that was one of the good things that she could see coming out of her divorce. James wasn't a great husband. He hadn't supported her at all, had taken advantage of her support and the work that she had done to make their house a beautiful and welcoming home, and hadn't felt any need to do anything other than throw money at her. Which, of course she appreciated. Who didn't appreciate a comfortable lifestyle, without having to worry about whether or not the bills were being paid?

But as for a man who she could share a love story with, James really wasn't that good. He would rather golf on Saturday mornings than spend his day off with her. And she could go on and on. There really wasn't too much that he'd not rather do than spend time with her. In fact, even before he announced that he was leaving her and before he said he was with someone else, she couldn't remember the last time they'd done something together, and it wasn't because she didn't want to. It was because of him.

The ladies had started talking again, no pressure on her to continue, and she appreciated it. The way they accepted her, the way they told her that they understood about divorce, and that it was hard and that it would take time to come to grips with things, made her feel almost overwhelmed at the amount of love and acceptance being poured out.

They took a break after about forty-five minutes so the snacks could be refilled, since there was a limited amount of room on the coffee table, and during the break, Skyler pulled Shannon aside.

"I know I told you that I had my own story, and all the ladies here have already heard how I was abandoned. My fiancé just drove away without me. In fact, it wasn't somewhere random. It was here at Fran's. I wandered over trying to find some shelter for the night, and I went into labor. That's how far along I was."

"Oh my goodness. Your boyfriend was a monster."

"He wasn't a good guy, that's for sure. But if it hadn't been for that, I wouldn't have met Homer. Who *is* a good guy. And out of that—the pain of being abandoned when I was carrying another man's baby and so close to giving birth, when he should have been protecting me and making sure that I was okay—something beautiful was born. I think God specializes in writing beautiful endings from broken beginnings. At least He did in my story. Or maybe He just specializes in making anything that's broken beautiful." Skyler was smiling and seemed to glow with happiness. There was no doubt that God had given her a happy ending to her love story.

"Did Homer adopt your baby?"

Skyler nodded. "He fell in love. He's raising her as his, and we have two more." She grinned. "He's gonna be a little frazzled when I get home this evening, but he loves them—there's just no doubt."

Homer didn't look like the kind of guy who got frazzled, but Skyler would know.

The group reconvened shortly after that, and Mertie gave some more teaching from the Bible. Shannon just drank it up, like this was the first water she'd had in weeks. She just couldn't get enough and was shocked to see that it was ten o'clock when Mertie said that it was time to draw to a close. They prayed together, and Mertie prayed for all of the prayer requests that had been shared during the evening, including Shannon's new start and the work at the inn, and her words were so sincere and so comforting and so amazing that Shannon nearly started to cry on the spot.

As she said goodbye to the ladies, Vera offered to walk her out. Shannon wanted to decline, but Vera already had a hand on the doorknob.

"I appreciate it. Everyone was so welcoming, and I just had such an amazing time. Mertie is a natural Bible teacher," Shannon said as they walked down the walk.

"She really is. Every time she speaks, I just get so much out of it."

"I'm looking forward to next week already."

"I look forward to it every week. It's a night off, a night to fellowship and grow closer, but it's also good food and friends too."

"I can only imagine. The food was delicious."

They took a couple of steps without either one of them saying anything, and then Vera, in a very casual voice, said, "Lance has been asking me about you. He wanted to make sure that I had invited you, which of course, I already had, but...not prying, just wanted to let you know that he's concerned and interested. If you have anything you want to share, I have a reputation for being able to keep my mouth shut."

"Well, good to know. Although... I don't know that I have anything to say about Lance right now." She had a whole lot she was thinking about him, but nothing that she'd even admitted to herself. Not the attraction, not the memories that had been buried that made her feel like she had made the absolute wrong choice, and not the way she felt bad for breaking her promise.

"He's a good man. He's been waiting a long time for the right woman. I... He didn't say this, but I kind of feel like he thinks it might be you."

Shannon's breath caught. Really? She wouldn't be just saying that, would she?

She didn't know what to say, so she put a foot in front of the other one and continued to walk.

"No pressure. I just wanted to say something. I also wanted to make sure that you knew that my offer of designing any kind of healing space you wanted, whether inside or out, was open, and Dominic will build whatever I design. Just let me know."

"Thank you so much. There actually is a small spot in the back where I thought a patio would be nice. The view isn't as good, but it would be a good place to go and just sit and enjoy. That might be a really great place for not a healing garden exactly but just a healing spot."

"Sounds great. I'll come and check it out sometime this week."

"And there is a room downstairs, it used to be a conference room, I think, and I suppose I could still use it for that, but I was thinking that you might be able to do something in there, to make people feel welcome and encouraged."

"I'd love to. I'll take a look at that while I'm there as well."

"Thanks again for the invitation. Just being here tonight has made me feel so good. And knowing that these ladies are my friends and neighbors has eased my mind considerably."

"It's not easy to move by yourself to an entirely new spot, even if it was the town you grew up in. It's changed a lot since you left."

"It certainly has, and you're right. It's been a lot harder than I even anticipated, and I never thought it was going to be easy."

"Just remember, we're all here for you."

Vera gave her a hug, and Shannon was hard-pressed to let go. She wanted to hold on and simply enjoy the feeling of being surrounded by someone who loved and cared for her.

But they pulled back and said good night, and Shannon got in her car and drove away, considerably happier as she left than what she was when she came.

It had also been very good for her to see that everyone else had painful times that they went through, and to see God's grace and God's goodness in each of their lives, how He'd taken the hard times and turned them into something amazing. It gave her the feeling that if He could do it for them, maybe He would do it for her too.

Nine

"Can we talk to you for a minute?" Dominic stuck his head in the door where Shannon and Lance were working.

"Sure, Dominic. Do you want to come in here?" Shannon asked, glancing at Lance, who did not seem surprised to see Dominic.

"Sure. This will be fine. Do you mind if we sit down on the buckets? It might be an extensive conversation."

Shannon had no idea what he might want to talk about, although there were plenty of things to discuss as there was tons of work to do on the inn. And they were only getting started.

She made herself comfortable as the men sat down and only glanced at Lance once. He didn't seem to be trying to look innocent, and he didn't seem to avoid her eyes either.

She stopped trying to guess what he might or might not know, and what he might or might not have told her, and just watched Dominic.

"I told you when we started that I would be doing an extensive assessment of the electrical and plumbing systems in the inn. There's no point in patching drywall if we only have to take it apart in order to rewire or replumb things. Things like closets and windows are fine to take care of immediately, since there's typically no electricity in there.

Along with the roofing crew that is even now planning on totally redoing the roof starting tomorrow."

"Oh my goodness. I didn't realize it was going to happen so soon!" Shannon said, excited despite herself.

Part of her was terrified that Dominic was going to say that there was too much work to do and they just absolutely could not do it without a major check from her.

"The good news is the foundation is secure and in really good shape. I couldn't find a thing wrong with it, and I told Trevor and Josiah that as soon as they wanted to start redoing the porch, they could. I think they said they would order the material and start tearing the old one off immediately."

"Wow. Things are really happening," she said.

"Yeah. We can re-side the house when they have the porch off, and that should be done by the end of next week or possibly two weeks, depending on the weather. I... I really wanted to get as much done outside as we could before the weather gets bad. Snow could put an end to our work for a while."

"Do you think you can get it all done before the snow comes?" Shannon asked, realizing that they were closer to that than she wanted to admit.

"Yes. I think we can. As long as nothing unexpected comes up. I wouldn't have been able to say that until we did a thorough investigation into all of the other systems, but since the foundation is good, and the roof has not been leaking long enough to rot any of the rafters, I think we're in really good shape. Better shape than I would have hazarded to guess when we first looked at the inn."

"That's excellent news," she said, realizing that he had said that he was going to give her the good news first. By default, that meant there was bad news.

"Yes. And the bad news isn't terrible. Lance?"

"Oh, you get to deliver the good news, and I get to talk about the bad. Is that the way it goes?"

Dominic just laughed, and Shannon smiled, but her eyes narrowed. So Lance did know something, and he hadn't told her.

"Dominic asked me to go and look at the wiring and the plumbing. I have more experience in that than he does."

"Okay," she said, trying not to hurry him along. He could take his time and say what he wanted to.

"So the electrical system seems to have been replaced on the first and second floor, but on the third floor, it looks like about 1930s work."

"Oh."

"I actually don't know the year, I just know that it's not in good shape, and I feel the best thing to do—the safest thing—would be to totally rewire the entire third floor. The plumbing also could use some work, but if we're trying to get things done...by maybe the holidays?" He stopped and lifted his brows at Dominic and then at her.

"In my heart, I was kind of hoping we could have a soft launch at the beginning of November, but I didn't want to do that and push people. Especially people who are donating their time and a lot of materials. I am just grateful for whatever you can do."

"Well, rewiring the upstairs will be a big enough job for me. So we're going to hire out the plumbing. That might be something that you'll have to pay for, although Dominic and I haven't come to a firm decision on that."

"What he's trying to say is both of us can do it, but neither one of us are sure that we have the time. If we're trying to open anytime soon, it would be best to hire out. So basically you have a choice—do you want to pay for it and have it take a shorter time? Or are you okay with Lance and I doing it together, knowing it just might take a little bit of extra time?"

"While you're doing the third story, the first and second story can be completed and rented out?" she asked.

This is where she wished she had someone to talk to. These were decisions that she wasn't used to making on her own. It was times like these where she felt the most alone and vulnerable.

"That's exactly right. You could—we can focus on the first and second story and get those done. I believe Lance would be best served by starting the wiring, and then he'll be available to help with the plumbing as well on the third story."

"Okay."

"I was assuming that you would be able to help me," Lance said. He lifted his brows and waited for her answer.

What Vera had said the night before came back to her. Something about Lance being interested in her. Was it possible? Or, was he really in need of a helper and she was the only one who could be spared?

"I have no experience in wiring anything." She felt like that would be the honest thing to say.

Lance chuckled. "I really didn't think you did. But I don't need someone with experience. I need someone who can grab tools for me, get things that I need, hold things, and just be a general right-hand man for me. You don't have to have any experience. That will save us from taking someone else off a different crew and putting them to work on the third floor, which will make it take longer to get the first two floors done."

"Well then, of course. Yes, absolutely I'll help you, and let's do that. We'll save the money, and you guys can do it. If that's okay with you?" She didn't want to put them out. But she couldn't tell from what they had said whether they actually wanted to do it or were just doing it because they felt like they had to, now that they'd volunteered for it. "If you have other work that's pressing..."

"I don't," Dominic said immediately.

"Neither do I. Tyler is at the store, and I've already spoken with him. He's perfectly fine working as much as I need him to."

"As long as you guys are okay with it, I'm in. And I'll help you." That was an easy decision—she wished they were all that easy.

"All right then. I'll manage the crews to get the first floor done first and then the second floor. We might even be able to open the first floor at the beginning of November. I'll try to figure some things out and give you a solid date later this week."

"Perfect. I don't need a whole lot of advance warning, but once I know that I can put it up and start advertising, I'll do that." She had a little bit of experience in advertising, although not much. She'd worked for an agency for a while once the kids were in school.

"All right, I'll work on making at least one room picture-perfect so you can have some photos for your ads." Dominic stood from the bucket where he had sat down.

"I appreciate that."

"Sure. And I'll try to keep an eye on things, and when I'm sure that you can count on an opening date, I'll let you know."

"Sounds good. As soon as I know for sure what I can count on, I'll start trying to sell rooms."

"Sounds good." He said a few more things to Lance before he walked out of the room.

"Are you sure you're okay with that?" Lance asked in his normal, considerate way. Not only was he one of the nicest people that Shannon knew, she enjoyed watching him work, seeing how capable he was with his hands. He had always been good with them, and she remembered admiring him in high school for the exact same thing. He was quiet, but his expertise and competence was attractive, and anytime she had any questions, he was always happy to explain as little or as much as she wanted. He didn't treat her like she didn't know anything, nor did he act like he was superior to her because he did. He just made it seem natural that they were working together and she was learning. She had never worked with anyone she enjoyed working with more.

"How much of that did you know?" she asked as he stood up and gathered up some of his tools.

"I had to give my report to Dominic, because he had asked me to check the electrical systems. So I felt like it was important that I answered to him. And I wasn't sure what he was going to decide. I didn't want to get the cart ahead of the horse. Not to mention, you can't really have two bosses for one job. He's the boss of this job, and it would be a little bit inconsiderate of me to jump ahead and talk to you without the actual boss coming to you."

She understood what he was saying. And it made sense. How could she be upset with him for just being respectful to Dominic and his position?

"But it looks like we're moving up to the third floor. I need to look around, and if you don't mind making a list, we'll figure out exactly what we need to get started."

"I don't mind at all. Anything I can do to help move this project along is something I'm absolutely willing to do. As long as I don't get in your way."

He stopped and turned. She could feel his gaze the whole way to her toes. "You've never been in the way."

She nodded and smiled and said, "Well, I'll take your word for it, but it's hard to believe. You've been very patient and sweet with me, and I appreciate it."

They went around and gathered up their things, and did not talk about anything more personal for the rest of the morning as they looked at the third floor, and she made notes as he went through and did some figuring.

Everyone else ate lunch before they were through, and they ended up sitting out on the porch together with the meatloaf and scalloped potatoes that Marina had held back for them, which was still warm.

"Such a beautiful day," Shannon said as she lifted her face to the lake breeze. This was why she wanted to come back. This glorious view, the fresh air, the feeling of community and of being supported by people who truly liked and cared about her.

And Lance. She hadn't come back for Lance. Not on purpose anyway. But maybe, subconsciously she had known all along that she had missed the one that she had been meant for.

"It sure is. It's the kind of day like this that makes you happy that you're alive, that you live by the lake, makes you feel blessed."

"I definitely feel blessed," she agreed, closing her eyes and savoring the delicious food and the feel of the wind on her face.

"Do you ever wonder about the road not taken?" he asked her, causing her to open her eyes in surprise.

He looked thoughtful, and his gaze was out on the lake as he put a bite of food in his mouth and chewed slowly.

"I suppose I do. I suppose I do wonder what might have happened if...things had been different."

"Care to elaborate on that?" he asked casually, looking down at his plate as he forked another bite onto his utensil.

"I suppose we all have choices that we make that we regret," she said, not sure she was ready to talk about their past specifically. She owed him an apology, but she hadn't really thought too much about what she was going to say, and she didn't want to bungle it too badly. "What about you? Do you have roads you wish you would have taken?"

"I suppose. In some ways. But I can't help but think that God has moved everything that I've done so that things would work out the way He wanted them to. Just my thoughts."

"God does have a way of moving things around and making things work out. At Bible study, they were talking about how He makes beautiful things out of broken things, and I think that's true."

Neither one of them said anything more for a while as they finished their meal in silence.

"I don't know what you're doing for supper tonight, but if you don't have any plans, I was kind of hoping you'd come over and share a meal with me. I'd like for you to meet my sister."

Lance broke the silence with a request she was not expecting. Still, just because she wasn't expecting it didn't mean that she didn't say yes immediately.

"I'd love to." Marina had two nights off a week, and tonight happened to be one of them. It wasn't that it was that hard to warm up leftovers, but it would be nicer to eat with Lance and his sister. "As I recall, she was in an accident not long before I left?"

"I think it was about three years before you left. But yeah, she was in an accident and barely survived. She...is developmentally delayed, I guess is what it's called. Basically, she's in her mid-thirties but has the mental abilities of about a ten-year-old. The docs said she would never get any better, and they were right. As much as I wished it was different over the years. It was hard to see her never be able to get married or have a family of her own."

"And you gave up everything in order to stay and take care of her?" Shannon said slowly.

Lance didn't say anything, but he tilted his head a little as though acknowledging her words. It was true, from what Shannon could remember. His mother had died, and his dad had his hands full, trying to manage the hardware store and take care of his sister at the same time.

"What was her name again?" she asked.

"It's Katie, and she's eager to meet you."

"She is?" Shannon asked, surprised Katie even remembered her.

"I might have been talking about you some. I think she might have been a little bit young to remember that you and I were a thing."

"I see," she said softly.

"Yeah. Anyway—"

"Actually, now that I'm thinking about it, your mother died when Katie was born, and you stayed to help raise her."

"That's true. I thought when she turned eighteen, I would be free of my responsibility, because I promised my mom that I would help my dad before she passed away. Once Katie was off on her own, I felt like I would be free to pursue a degree in electrical engineering. That's what I had always wanted to do. But God had other plans."

"I see." She had totally forgotten about that. She loved what that said about him. The sacrifice, the way he put his family first. That he would sacrifice what he wanted for the good of someone else. For his sister who needed him.

"And your dad had a heart attack?" she asked, trying to remember the gossip that she'd heard.

"Yeah. Not long after Katie's accident. I might have left anyway, if it hadn't been for that. But I took over the hardware store, and Katie and I have been living pretty happily ever since."

His eyes shifted to her, and they looked at each other for a moment before he looked away again.

She couldn't help but think that things might have been different if she hadn't broken her promise to him and if they had ended up married. His life would have been...maybe happier? She wasn't sure. He didn't seem to be upset with her or upset with the way his life turned out. He didn't even seem resigned, just content. Hadn't he just said that God had a way of working things out?

"All right, I better get back to work, but I just want to make sure that we're on for tonight."

"We sure are. Tell me what time you want me and what I should bring."

"You don't need to bring anything. I've become a fair cook over the years, and we just want your company. That's all."

She gathered their things up and took his dirty plate from him so she could drop it off in the kitchen while he went up to get started working. She was careful not to let their fingers brush. She had found out some things about him today that made him even more appealing than he already had been. And she would be hard-pressed to keep her distance. But that was what she needed to do.

Ten

Shannon stood on the porch of Lance's house, waiting for him to answer the door. She was unaccountably nervous, especially since she and Lance worked together so well, and she felt more at home with him than she did with anyone she knew, except for possibly her children.

Still, she couldn't deny the fact that her hands were sweaty and butterflies tangled in her stomach.

Surely, once he opened the door and she saw his face, she would calm right down, but... For some reason, she wanted him to...like her? He already did. She wasn't worried about that. Not really. But she had showered and carefully styled her hair, and even applied a little makeup, which she hadn't been wearing at all around the inn. She wore a flattering skirt and a shirt that hugged her curves. She was as dressed up as she ever got, and she was hoping that...it was enough? That she was enough? Was she still wondering whether she was enough?

"Good evening," Lance said as he opened the door.

"Is this her? Is this the girl you've been talking about?" Katie stood beside him, her attitude and words that of a ten-year-old, but the body and face of a woman in her mid-thirties. It was an odd combination, and Shannon was only able to blink.

"I think we're overwhelming her. But yes, this is Shannon. Shannon, this is my sister, Katie. She's excited," Lance said, patting Katie's head like she was much younger than the mid-thirties that she had to have been.

"It's very nice to meet you, Katie."

"Lance talks about you all the time. He says he used to have the biggest crush on you."

"Katie," Lance said, warning in his tone, although patience in his voice too.

"I used to have a really big crush on him as well... We were together for a while. But then I left."

"I know. He's not mad at you though. And he really wants me to like you. Which I know I'm going to."

"And I know I'm going to like you," Shannon said as Lance led the way inside, and Katie wrapped her arm with Shannon's and walked beside her.

"Lance is the best big brother in the world. Although he does make me go to bed early. Eight o'clock, can you believe it?"

"Wow. Sometimes I go to bed at eight o'clock. Sometimes I go to bed at 7:30," Shannon said. She'd always been an early to bed and early to rise kind of person.

"Sometimes I just need a little bit of peace and quiet, and Katie's awesome, but she never stops talking," Lance said, lifting a brow at Katie, who giggled.

"That's true. Lance always says I chatter like a magpie. I really don't know what a magpie is, and he hasn't been able to tell me, so I think he's just making it up."

"You should Google it."

"Oh, I'm not allowed to have a phone. Lance says I can get myself into too much trouble with it."

Shannon nodded and wondered about that. Maybe it had something to do with her developmental delay—she wasn't sure. But Katie was charming and sweet, and it was so nice to see Lance's gentle care with her.

"It looks like you forgot to set a third plate, Katie," Lance said gently.

Katie put a hand over her mouth and gasped. "I was so excited to have visitors, and I totally forgot to even set you a plate!"

"We can pretend it was my plate that you forgot," Lance suggested.

"But you sit at the head of the table, and your plate's there. I want to put Shannon right beside you, so I'm going to put her across the table from me. That way, she's close to you." Katie giggled.

Shannon knew her cheeks were bright red, because she could feel the heat.

As she looked at Lance, his cheeks were flushed under his tan as well.

Katie was so joyful, so full of life and fun and happiness that Shannon was charmed by her. She totally accepted Shannon and gave several uninhibited statements about how she would like for her brother to get married and that Shannon was the perfect girl for him. At least from what Lance had said.

By the time the meal was over, Shannon absolutely loved Katie, and Lance was absolutely embarrassed beyond words.

Still, his patience and love for his sister was obvious.

"It's your turn for the dishes, but since you also helped to make the meal, I think I should help you."

"I can help dry," Shannon offered, after Lance spoke.

"I think it's a good idea to have help sometimes," Katie said, giggling again. "And do I get to stay up later tonight too?"

"Absolutely not. You have a big day tomorrow, because you're going to Sierra's house. It's always a lot of fun there, and you come back exhausted. So you need to get a good night's rest."

"Oh. I forgot. Sierra lives just outside of town on a farm. Three days a week, I get to go to her house and help. She has goats and rabbits and a bunch of kids too. And she lets me come and play with the kids and help her with the animals. I do some cleaning too," Katie said, rattling off what she did while ticking the things off on her fingers.

"That sounds like a lot of fun," Shannon said. "I can see why you'd be tired at the end of the day."

"I am not tired. Lance just worries."

"I see. Big brothers are like that, aren't they?"

"They are. Sometimes they're a real pain in the butt." The way Katie said it was so endearing that Shannon had to laugh.

The dishes were soon done, and they played a couple of games at the table before it was time for Katie to go get ready for bed.

"If you don't mind, we could have some dessert out on the porch as soon as Katie is settled for the night," Lance said.

"I don't mind at all."

It wasn't long after that that Lance came down the stairs, stepping softly.

"She always falls asleep right as soon as her head hits the pillow. Sometimes I wish that I could be that innocent and totally carefree. Because I'll lay awake thinking about things for hours some nights."

"Same," she said, thinking that it would be nice in some ways to be like Katie, joyful, happy, giggling over everything with not a care in the world, but... "Not everyone is blessed enough to have a big brother who will put their life on hold or completely derail it in order to take care of them." She wanted to tell him how much she admired that. How impressed she was at how selfless he was. But the words just wouldn't come.

"I guess I didn't have a choice."

"You sure did. She could have gone to an institution. You could have given her over to the state or something."

"I suppose I could have. But I just couldn't have done that. Even now, I worry sometimes about what's going to happen to her when something happens to me."

"Do you have things set up for her?"

"I do. And I have some money put back that will hopefully pay for it all."

"Is Sierra a babysitter?" she asked carefully. Lance didn't seem like he was easily offended, but especially when a person was talking about family, one never knew.

"Yes. She is. She keeps her three days a week, and then I have another neighbor who keeps her too. We don't really say that she's being babysat, but that's what it is. Not that she couldn't stay home by herself, and if I have to work on the weekend, she does. She's old enough to— she just... I don't want her to be home by herself all day long every day. And friends for someone like her are kind of few and far between. It's weird seeing a grown woman act like a ten-year-old."

"It did take me aback a little bit, but she's so sweet and just innocently joyful that you can't help but fall in love with her."

Lance pulled a pie out of the refrigerator. "I had Lauren make this special for us. It's blueberry."

Shannon's hand stopped as she reached for the drawer to get some forks. "You remembered."

"Of course," he said, like it was the most natural thing in the world for him to remember her favorite kind of pie. They had a conversation about it that had been brought back as soon as he said blueberry. About how Michigan was known for their blueberries, and blueberry pie was her absolute favorite, but she hardly ever got it because she couldn't make pies that didn't run all over the place.

"We'll have to see if this one's runny or not," Lance said with a grin.

"I can't believe you remembered." James would never have remembered anything like that. Honestly, she couldn't trust James to remember something that she said two hours before, let alone two decades.

She supposed that was what happened when someone really liked someone else. Was interested in them. They were interested in everything and wanted to know everything there was to know about them.

He cut two pieces and pulled them out without it running anywhere. "Lauren said if you let it cool, it has a tendency to not be as runny."

"I wonder if I knew that back then."

"Maybe that's why you could never get them to turn out the way you wanted them to. You were always too impatient to cut into them."

"If I recall correctly, anytime you knew that I was making a blueberry pie, you were there with bells on well before I brought it out of the oven."

"You do recall correctly," he said.

They grinned at each other, and then he turned to get ice cream out of the freezer while she put the pies in the microwave for a few seconds each.

Finally, when their desserts were ready, they walked out on the porch.

"Do you want to sit on the swing?" Lance asked, nodding toward where it swayed gently in the lake breeze at the end of the porch.

"I'd love to. We spent lots of evenings chatting on the swing."

"We sure did," Lance said, glancing at her but not saying anything more.

They walked over and sat down together, the springs creaking slightly under their weight.

"It's so impressive the way you take care of Katie. The obvious love that you have for her, the patience you show her. No wonder you're so patient with me while we're working together."

"You're a lot different than Katie," he said, and he gave her a look that said in more ways than one.

She didn't know what to say to that, so she didn't say anything.

"She's all the family I have. Of course I love her. Of course I'd be patient with her. I love her." He lifted his shoulder, like it was that simple.

"It's not that easy. There are a lot of people who would not have sacrificed what you did in order to take care of a sister who could have been sent to an institution. They might not have been able to wait to get rid of her. And yet... You rearranged your entire life. I love that. It's beautiful."

"I don't know if it's beautiful or not. But I guess I just don't feel like I wanted to make any other choice. It wasn't a hard one. I mean, sure, I was looking forward to getting out of the house when she was born. And when my mom was dying, I promised her that I would take care of her. I promised I wouldn't leave Dad alone."

"Do you really think your mom expected you to keep that promise?"

"I've wondered that over the years. If she would have known that she was making me promise that the next eighteen years of my life, I wouldn't go anywhere." He paused for a moment. "I wanted to follow you to college. Sometimes I wonder...if I would have gone...if things would have been different."

He was saying he wanted to know if he would have gone, whether she would have kept her promise if he'd been right in front of her.

"I owe you an apology. I gave you a promise, and I broke it. Maybe that's why I admire what you did so much."

"No. You don't owe me an apology. We were what? Seventeen? You didn't know what you wanted to do with your life. And then you went to college, and I stayed here. You didn't know what I was going to do, whether I would be able to support a family without an education. I don't blame you at all."

"You're more magnanimous than most people would be."

"I don't know about that," Lance said, and she realized something else—he was humble too.

"Still, when Katie turned eighteen, you could have dumped her on someone else."

"No. I couldn't. I just wouldn't have. It wouldn't sit right with me."

"You realize that you're fifty years old, and you've never left this town because of your sister."

"Is it because of my sister?"

She stared at him.

"Or is it because of God? Because of the way He worked in my life? Maybe it was His will that I stay here. That I take care of her, and that I needed to grow and become more like Jesus by taking care of Katie, by giving up what I wanted, by not being bitter and angry about it, by not resenting the fact that she had maybe 'stolen' from me what someone else would have thought that I deserved. I... I'm a different person than I used to be. And it's all because of her. And the way God has worked in my life."

"Wow. That's such a mature and spiritual way of looking at things." She hadn't even thought about it like that, but it was kind of the conclusion that she had been trying to come to about her divorce. That God was allowing the trial in her life in order to make her a stronger, better person. She wanted to believe that, but in order for that to happen, she had to choose not to be bitter and angry but to choose forgiveness and love and joy and peace. All the things that seemed to come so easily to Lance.

"I suppose the one thing I do regret is that...when you came back, you were married. And I'd obviously missed my chance. If... If there was one thing I could change, it would have been to chase after you, but...

I'm not sure that that would have been the wise thing to do. After all, you needed to make your own choice, and you didn't choose me."

"I should have," she said, and her words hung softly in the night air.

She shouldn't have said them. She shouldn't have let him know that she regretted that choice—all those years ago—to break up with him and to pursue something else, to allow James to develop a relationship with her. It was the worst mistake of her life. But ever since she'd come back to Raspberry Ridge, it seemed like the Lord had been trying to teach her that He could make beautiful things out of broken things, He could make joy and gladness come from mistakes.

"You're just as beautiful now as you were then," he said, and his hand came up, brushing her hair away.

She leaned closer, and his breath whispered across her skin.

It felt perfect and right the same way it had all those years ago. Except her ex-husband was between them, and Lance wasn't anything like him, and maybe that was what jolted her out of her trance, because she moved, dropping her fork on the floor with a clatter.

"Oh goodness. It's late, I need to go." She jumped up from the swing and almost got hit in the head with it as she leaned down to pick up the fork. "Thank you so much for the meal and the company, everything was really nice, but I have to run."

She shoved her plate and fork at him, and he took it, but she could tell by the look on his face, he was confused.

Whether he was confused about how she felt, confused about why she was leaving so fast, or just confused because she was obviously confused, she didn't know. And she didn't take the time to tell him. She just knew that she needed to get away. Even though a part of her was saying that she was running again.

Eleven

Shannon still hadn't fully recovered from her evening with Lance. She managed to work with him all day without having any kind of personal conversation, but she was unable to shut her brain off, so after supper, when Marina went to her room, Shannon continued to work. She was getting pretty good at spackling drywall, although she had been spending the last few days helping Lance with the electrical work.

Still, there was always something to do, and she would rather keep her hands busy and her mind occupied with what she was doing.

She was so involved in her work that it took her a while to realize that thunder had been slowly getting closer and closer, until lightning flashed and thunder crashed almost immediately afterward.

A storm was upon them.

She thought immediately of the tarp that was outside, covering some of the work that the guys had been doing, and hoped that they had realized that there was going to be a storm and had tied it down.

She figured that it was one of those lake storms that would blow through pretty quickly, and so she went back to work. A couple more crashes of thunder and flashes of lightning, and then the lights flickered.

No. The lights couldn't possibly go out.

She hadn't finished that thought when they flickered again, and the entire room went dark.

Thankfully, she had her phone and its flashlight and was able to put her tools in some semblance of order as the wind whipped at the windows, rattling them, and rain pounded—it almost sounded like there might have been some sleet or hail or something mixed in with it.

She thought about checking on Marina, but if Marina was sleeping, she didn't want to wake her.

In her experience, since Marina had come, once she went to her room, she didn't come out. She had a feeling that Marina slept like the dead.

Which would have been a nice thing to be able to do on a night like tonight. Then she wouldn't realize that the lights had gone out and that the wind was blowing so strongly it shook the entire structure.

Suddenly she heard glass crashing from the downstairs room that they were finishing for the pictures. It was the one that was the most done, and even though Shannon could barely see by the light of her phone, she went running to it. Thankfully, she didn't trip on anything, and she was able to get there in time to see that she needed to do something fast or the rain was going to ruin the drywall they had just installed. Of course, somebody was going to have to do something about the broken glass, but it looked like the frame of the window was good, the little she could see with her phone. Frantically, she started to dig around for the tarp or the plastic that she knew had been stored somewhere since they were painting in different areas of the inn.

She had no idea how she was going to hold it up herself, and again she thought about waking Marina, but she just couldn't bring herself to do it. The poor woman worked ceaselessly from the time she got up in the morning until the time she went to bed at night, and Shannon couldn't ask her to do more.

Then, she saw lights—headlights bouncing over the rough blacktop of the parking lot below.

Who could be here this time at night?

The inn was practically deserted, and now they had no electricity. Why hadn't she thought about this before?

But then, she saw a light pop on and could see from the glow that it was Lance.

From the flash of another strike of lightning, it looked like his strong nose, and she thought she recognized his hat as well. He jumped out of the truck and went running for the front door. She hurried out of the room and was there to open it when he got there so he didn't have to stand in the rain. The front porch wasn't finished, and the tarp was blowing wildly, threatening to blow off.

"Maybe you can come out and give me a hand with this tarp," Lance said in lieu of a greeting.

"Maybe you can help me in this room first. The drywall is in danger of getting soaked."

"Oh no," he said, stepping further in and closing the door behind him. She turned and hurried to the door to the room.

With two of them, they got the window sealed off in hardly any time.

"I don't even know where that branch could have come from," Lance said. "Do you mind coming out in the rain? You're probably going to get soaked. But I'm not sure I can get this tarp held down by myself."

"Yeah. I can come. I would have thought the storm would have blown itself out by now."

"Same. But when our lights went off at the house, I immediately thought of you guys and wanted to come out and check on everything."

"I appreciate it. I admit I had a few moments of total fear as I thought about how remote we are, and the idea of no electricity... I know it's silly, but it's scary."

"Don't worry about it. I can stay. I gave Sierra a call, and she was going to send her oldest daughter out to stay at the house with Katie."

"Oh. Wow, okay." Shannon didn't know what to say. He actually had already made plans to spend the night and make sure that they were okay. It was really sweet of him.

"You ready?" he asked before he opened the door. She nodded. And they rushed out into the windy night together. Using their phones as flashlights, they were able to get the tarp secured and had just started back toward the house when a tree branch from the large tree at the front of the inn crashed down, breaking the dining room window.

"Come on. It's too dangerous to stay here. Let's go sit in my pickup until the storm's blown out. The dining room hasn't been touched anyway," Lance yelled above the storm, and Shannon caught pretty much every other word. Enough to know that they were running for his truck. That, and the fact that he grabbed her hand and started in that direction, gave her all the information she needed.

He went directly to the driver side and opened the door, helping her in. She slid across the seat, not bothering to try to move her legs around the shifter and things in the middle. He got in and slammed the door behind him, and they sat there for a moment, soaking wet and panting.

"I'm sorry that you got all wet because of me and my inn."

"I think everybody in town has a stake in this inn. I'm certainly not the only one that wants to see you succeed." He looked down at her, and the tender look in his eyes belied his casual words. "Plus, I'm not gonna leave you out here by yourself."

She looked around and then realized that maybe she should slide over some. They were cramped together, like teenagers on a date night.

"I'm trying to get myself untangled so I can get my feet on the other side of this thing." She pointed to the shifter on the floor of the truck. It must have been a 1980s model or something like that, and she vaguely remembered Lance fixing up vehicles in his spare time. He said he wasn't any good at it, but he must have been not terrible if he had something this old still running.

"You're fine where you are," Lance said. "I don't know about you, but I'm a little chilly."

"I am too. Maybe you should start the pickup so we can get a little heat from the heater." She wasn't going to just sit there, and she worked on trying to get her feet around the shifter without knocking anything important.

They got themselves adjusted, and he got the truck started. Eventually, warm air started to come out.

"This brings back memories," she said finally.

"It does," he said.

They sat there in silence for a while as the air from the heater blew and they began to dry out while the storm continued unabated.

Maybe it was the dark, maybe it was the cozy feeling inside of the cab, but Shannon felt more secure than she had in the daylight. And she wanted to explain, to let him know why she had been so skittish the other night on the porch.

But for her, it started well before that night.

"After my husband cheated on me and left me, he made it clear that he was choosing her over me. It was hard to believe that he would leave a three-decade marriage and our two children in favor of some woman he had just met, who he didn't have any history with, didn't have any kids with. And it made me feel...like I wasn't enough."

"You're more than enough," Lance said softly but fiercely.

She ignored him. "I felt like I was lost. Because my kids were done with college. They were going on to find jobs of their own, start their own lives, and here I was selling everything and having to start over again. I just felt like I didn't have anything to hold onto. And I hated that feeling. That feeling of losing my identity now that I was no longer a wife and no longer a mother." She'd felt terrible. Like if she were skinnier or prettier or had been a better wife, somehow, although she really didn't know how she could have done that, but if she had, her husband would have loved her enough to stay.

"I just questioned a lot of things. One of the things I questioned was the choice that I made all those years ago to take your promise ring off and put it in my pocket and walk away from you. If I'm being honest, that was the worst decision of my life."

"Shannon," Lance said, his voice tender. His arm came up and lay across the back of the seat, his fingers just touching the hair on her ear, pushing it back.

She wanted to lean into his hand, to borrow from his strength. "Lance, there's something about why I left town, about what happened. Something I should have told you."

Just then, a flash of lightning hit, and it had to have hit something in the yard, because there was a huge crack and immediately thunder crashed, shaking the pickup as they sat.

Shannon almost thought that the inn would be catching on fire and burning up before their very eyes, and she knew they would have to go in and get Marina. Hopefully that terrible crash didn't awaken her.

Somehow she had jumped when the lightning flashed, and she was closer to Lance than she had been, almost cradled in his arm.

"Shannon," he said, his voice a caress that wrapped around her, making her feel warm and happy and so totally cared for. He had left his warm, safe, comfortable house, and the sister that he loved, to come work in the rain with her and to make sure that she was safe. She couldn't imagine James leaving anything that was comfortable to do anything kind for her. And she appreciated it so much. She put a hand on his cheek, feeling the roughness of his day's worth of beard under her fingers.

"Lance," she said softly.

Just then, another flash of lightning lit up the truck, and she saw the look in his eyes, which could only be labeled as absolute adoration, before thunder crashed, and it sounded like something exploded. When they looked over, the tree that had been in the front yard toppled to the ground, crashing with a loud sound that left no mistake that it was completely done for.

The moment was gone, and now Shannon had to deal with the fact that a lot of their hard work would probably be destroyed by the storm. Maybe people would lose interest and not be interested in rebuilding. She would have to discuss that with Dominic in the morning after they assessed the damages.

Twelve

The next morning, Shannon arrived in the kitchen, blurry-eyed and with the knowledge that there was a lot of work to be done that day, only to see Marina standing in the middle of the room, a thoughtful look on her face.

"Good morning," she said wearily, wondering if Marina had realized how bad the storm was. As far as Shannon knew, the other woman had never even woken up.

"That was quite a storm that went through last night. I slept through it all, but I saw the damage this morning when I got up."

Marina was always up before she was, and sometimes she was already cooking in the kitchen when Shannon walked in. It was early this morning, though.

"It was quite a storm. Thankfully, Lance came and helped me get everything tied down, although once the tree branch broke the dining room window, we retreated to his truck, and then that big old tree in the front yard fell, and I'm not sure what we're going to do."

"You could have gotten me up. I would have helped."

"I know. I hated to wake you, then Lance was here and I didn't need to."

Marina nodded. "I was wondering if you'd like me to whip up some breakfast for everyone."

"We don't have any electricity," Shannon said, wishing there was some way Marina could do it.

"There's a camp stove in the shed. I saw it the other day when I was looking through trying to find a Dutch oven. If it's okay with you, I can make a fire outside and get something mixed up. I'm guessing that the crew is going to be pretty hungry. Most of them might not have electricity, and they might be coming to work without anything to eat."

"Good thinking. If you don't mind, I would love it. Actually, we might be able to use some of the wood from the tree to make the fire." It would be soaked, but they could figure something out.

"You let me worry with that. If I can't find enough broken sticks, maybe someone will come with a chainsaw and give me a hand. You just get on with the things that you need to do. Okay?" Marina looked at Shannon with a smile.

Shannon had to thank God once more for Marina. She'd been a blessing more than once. "All right. Thank you."

They smiled at each other, and Shannon figured that maybe she ought to make sure that she allowed people to know how much she appreciated them.

"Marina?"

Marina turned and lifted her brows.

"I really appreciate you. I really have no idea what I would have done these last few days without you. Thank you so much."

"Of course. Sometimes I think we're sent at exactly the right time to exactly the right place, to do just what we've been learning how to do our whole lives." She lifted her shoulder. "There's nothing better than to feel like you're needed and wanted."

Even though it had been a bit since she arrived, Marina sometimes looked over her shoulder with fear on her face. And she checked her phone quite often with that same look of fear.

Shannon wished there was something she could do to help, but she'd asked Marina multiple times, and Marina had always demurred. Maybe Marina just didn't want to share, maybe she was embarrassed, or maybe it was something that would get people into trouble. Shannon couldn't discount that. But the idea that Marina could be some kind of criminal was almost laughable. She was such a conscientious employee, going over and above anything anyone would expect, like today. The idea that she could have done something criminally wrong was almost laughable.

The morning flew by fast, with everyone busy cleaning up the mess the storm had wrought. Chainsaws buzzed in the front yard, and hammers rang throughout the inn.

Just a couple of hours after Shannon had talked to Marina, she was called downstairs for brunch.

Marina had made eggs Benedict on the camp stove, and Shannon wasn't the only one who was deeply impressed.

As everyone had sat down to eat, after Lance had said a blessing, the door crashed open, and Mateo strolled in.

He looked frantic until his eyes landed on Marina. And then he seemed to calm down, drawing several relieved breaths.

Shannon had to hide her smile. It had been obvious to her since the first day she talked to Mateo about Marina that he had a bit of a crush on her.

"I was just here to check the storm damage. I had heard some rumors in town that there were some trees down and there was damage at the inn, and I wanted to make sure everyone was okay." He looked around the room at all the people who were sitting and eating.

"Help yourself to some eggs Benedict. They are amazing, and Marina made them on just a camp stove," Shannon said, watching as Mateo's eyes widened, and he looked exceptionally impressed. His gaze landed on Marina, and she met his gaze shyly before she looked down at her lap.

Marina set her plate aside as she got up and made a plate for Mateo.

People murmured in the background, but Shannon was watching as Marina handed Mateo his plate along with silverware. She watched their fingers brush and watched Marina's face look startled and then her cheeks redden.

Mateo seemed equally affected as he held the silverware and continued to try to get Marina to look at him.

It was cute to watch their interplay. But Shannon had to finish her meal quickly, because there were things at the store that she needed to go get.

When she walked into Fran's with the familiar bell jingling over top of her, and the familiar smells of cinnamon and freshly painted wood mixing with a bit of mildew and that old scent that buildings had, she breathed it in and then smiled. Fran looked up from arranging souvenirs on a shelf.

"Quite a storm last night, wasn't it?" Fran said.

"It sure was. It sent me to you this morning because we have a few things that we need to get in order to fix things up."

"I heard there was a tree down and some damage to the inn."

"There was." She had been so afraid that people would say that it wasn't worth redoing, but no one had said anything of the kind. In fact, everyone had come determined to get things fixed immediately. She had totally forgotten her fear in the hustle and bustle of all of the activity at the inn.

"So tell me," Fran said, coming over to stand beside Shannon as she looked at Fran's supply of thumbtacks.

"Yeah?" Shannon said, looking at Fran, considering her a friend.

"You have that mysterious chef. I've been hearing some things about her, and... I guess I'm just curious about her background. Do you know where she came from?"

"I don't have any idea," Shannon had to admit. "She's pretty tight-lipped about her past."

"Dominic had mentioned that he knew a few people who owned restaurants in Chicago and they might know of her, if you'd like me to pass her name along. Or talk to him about her."

"Why would I do that?" Shannon asked.

"Just checking out her background, making sure everything is on the up and up. She looks like a sweetheart, but references are always a good idea. Just from one business owner to another. I've had people that worked here that I would have sworn were clean as a whistle, who ended up walking off with stuff I couldn't afford to lose."

Shannon nodded. She really didn't think there was anything wrong with Marina, but Fran was right. She probably should get her checked out.

"I'll ask her tonight. I haven't probed too deeply, but it would be good to have something on file. She's not technically on payroll right now, so I'm not worried about that, per se, but when the time comes, I'm going to need to have something."

"Oh, definitely. You need to have an application on file that always includes references. Anyway, we don't have to go into it now, and I just want you to know that I haven't seen anything or heard anything at all negative about her. In fact, she seems like a really sweet girl—woman—but... She does seem a little bit afraid as well." Fran's voice lowered, and it seemed thoughtful as she said her last sentence.

Shannon couldn't argue with her. She'd noticed the same thing. Probably even more than Fran had, since she worked with Marina so much.

"Plus, it's possible that she's running from something, and... Depending on the situation, the town will want to protect her."

That made Shannon smile. The idea that Marina, who had only been there for a short time, was already someone the town loved and wanted to protect, just warmed her heart and soul to her very bones. She loved her small town.

"Thank you. I know that would make Marina really happy to hear that."

"Of course," Fran said. "Now, is there something I can help you find?" she asked, and Shannon showed her the shopping list. It was longer than usual, because of the storm, but Dominic and Lance had both seemed confident that they would be able to have the inn back in shipshape shortly and continue on with the work, continuing to aim for an early November soft launch.

The thought of which gave Shannon a little tingle of nervousness. Plus excitement. Plus fear. And the knowledge that she needed to get to work on her marketing plan.

She was thinking about that as she walked into the inn later. She delivered the supplies where they needed to go and found Marina sitting in the kitchen, writing something down in a notebook.

She had just noticed Marina glancing fearfully at her phone and then sigh, almost in relief, before she glanced up and jumped off her chair, shocked to see Shannon in the doorway.

"I'm sorry. You scared me," Marina said with a hand to her chest.

"I'm sorry…"

This seemed like the best time to talk to her about it, so before Shannon could second-guess herself, she said, "I can't help but notice that you seem to always be looking over your shoulder. Is there something I should know?"

Marina shook her head.

Shannon thought maybe she should take a slightly different tack. "I just talked to Fran, who told me that Dominic said that he could maybe check some references in Chicago. I actually need to have an application on file if I would ever put you on payroll."

"No. That's not necessary. I'm between stages in my career. I… I just…would prefer not." Marina's voice kind of trailed off, and Shannon could see she looked vulnerable and a little scared. All the protective instincts in Shannon came out, and she walked over and put an arm around Marina.

"All right. You don't have to talk to me about it, and maybe it's not smart on my part, but I trust you. You've been a huge blessing to me, like I said this morning. And if there's anything I can do to help you, just let me know."

"I appreciate that. It's been a long time since I felt this…safe."

Thirteen

Shannon watched as Emma's car pulled into the lot. A shiver of excitement wrapped around her ribs. She always enjoyed spending time with her children. There had never been a time when she hadn't.

She had to admit she was a little nervous. What would Emma think about the huge changes she'd made in her life?

Emma, being pragmatic and protective, might not think that she'd made the best choices.

She didn't want to allow her daughter to talk her out of what she had decided to do. After all, she had always been her daughter's biggest cheerleader, even when Emma hadn't always done everything she thought she should.

Emma's car came to a stop, and Shannon hurried over to it, enveloping Emma in a huge hug as soon as she got out of her car.

"I'm so glad to see you, Mom," Emma said as she hugged her back, just as tightly. They'd always been close, and the divorce had seemed to make them closer, even as Emma had pulled away, starting her own life.

At one point, Emma had volunteered to move back, to give up everything she'd started just to be with her mom and take care of her in her time of need, but Shannon had put on a brave face and told Emma in no uncertain terms that Emma was to go live her own life and if Shannon needed her, she would let her know.

"So what was it that you wanted to show me here?" Emma asked as they pulled away.

"This is it," Shannon said with a little bit of pride and a little bit of fear mixed together.

Emma stared with her mouth open. Obviously, she hadn't thought the inn behind them was the one that Shannon had talked about.

"Mom, there's a blue tarp covering half of it, the half that doesn't look like it's completely crumbling to the ground. And... Is that a broken window?"

They hadn't been able to get the window fixed. It was something that had to be special ordered and wasn't going to be in for a couple of weeks. They'd put clear plastic over it in the meantime.

"And the porch is a mess." Emma turned to face her and put a hand on both of her shoulders. "Please tell me the inside looks a lot different. Like it's not decrepit and doesn't look like it belongs in a 1980s horror movie."

Shannon bit her tongue. The inside was worse. "But can't you see the potential? Can't you see happy families going up and down the stairs, smiling and laughing and enjoying the lake view? Can't you see them having vacations the way we did? Making memories that will last a lifetime? I mean, don't you remember the vacations that we took when you were little?"

"Mom? You bought this because you wanted to give someone vacation memories like we have?" Emma looked like she was at a loss for words. "Mom! You could have bought a functioning inn. Not an inn that looks like it needs to be completely bulldozed and rebuilt."

Emma bit her lip, as though she knew she was crashing her mother's dreams to the ground. "I mean, it's your life, but..." she started out, sounding a little unsure of how she wanted to phrase it. Like she was drawing on the persuasive speech instruction she'd gotten in college to try to convince her mother that this was a really bad idea. "Are you sure you can handle this financially? I mean, this has to be a huge money pit. But more than that, Mom, emotionally are you capable of the stress? I mean, you've been through a lot in the last year. Shouldn't you go somewhere to rest and recover? This is definitely not going to help your emotional state."

Shannon listened and allowed Emma to talk. What else could she do? Her daughter was entitled to her opinion. "Why don't you walk in? Let's bring your stuff. I have a room set up for you." She was going to give Emma her room off the kitchen, since it was the nicest room in the inn so far. She planned to spend the next couple of nights in a room that was not finished at all and use the bathroom down the hall, sharing it with Marina.

"Is there a room in there that's not crumbling?" Emma asked, looking dubiously at the inn.

"You're going to love it. And I can see it clearly, the finished product, people happy, and yes, you're right. It's not going to be easy, but... I don't necessarily think that the easy way is the best way. And I don't think I taught you that growing up either. I mean, I guess we didn't have a terribly hard life, but that wasn't because we went around avoiding all the hard things."

"You're right. And you've always encouraged me to make the decision that was best, not easiest, but still... Mom, you're fifty. You're not young anymore."

Okay, that was hard. She was right, but it wasn't like Shannon woke up in the morning and looked in the mirror and told herself, "You're not young anymore, you can't do anything."

Fifty wasn't that terribly old. Sure, she was well past what would most likely be the midpoint of her life which was not something that she thought about very often. Instead, she wanted to keep her eyes focused on the things that she could do to be a blessing, to make her life count, to encourage and uplift others around her. She didn't want to be someone who just sat out the rest of her days catering to herself all the time. She didn't enjoy being around people who were only interested in making themselves happy. Why would she want to become a person like that?

She looped her arm through Emma's as they climbed the stairs together, Emma carrying a suitcase in her other hand, with a bag slung over her shoulder.

"I don't know how to explain it, other than I don't want to just sit back and let the rest of my life pass me by while I'm focused on enjoying it, you know? I want to have a purpose. This is a purpose for me. And you're right, it might fail, but... That's okay. Failure isn't the end. It's just one way that didn't work."

Emma looked down before she raised her head and met Shannon's gaze. "I suppose you're right, Mom. You always told me that in college too and even in high school when things didn't work out. Like losing a friendship isn't the end of the world, even though it feels like it at the time. Or losing a boyfriend. Same deal. And you were always right. You always told me to look for the lessons. But, Mom. Wow."

It seemed like Emma was coming around a little bit. But Shannon didn't give her a long tour of the inn. Instead, once Emma put her things in the room, she said, "Why don't we go check out the town? It's been a while since you've been here, and there have been some big changes. And people are so wonderful and welcoming, I know they're going to enjoy meeting you."

"All right, Mom. You've always had such a positive spin on things. I'm glad to see that you seem to be coming out of the divorce depression you were in for a while."

Had she been in a divorce depression? She hadn't even realized that Emma thought she had. Or that she had a name for it. What a depressing name.

"Tell me about what's going on with you," she said as they walked back down the steps. She tucked her hand in her daughter's arm. "I hope it's okay if we walk to town? It's only about ten minutes."

"Ten minutes? Tell me there are more houses than what I passed when I drove here?" Emma said. "That's another thing, Mom. You're out in the middle of nowhere."

"It's only a ten-minute walk to town. Far less if you drive it." She did not mention that they had been without electricity for two days the past week after a bad storm. That definitely wasn't going to be put in the positive column for Emma.

They turned away from the inn and began to walk toward town. "Tell me about your job and your apartment and your life. I feel like we have so much catching up to do. And Brian, what's going on with him?"

Emma smiled. "We're just taking it slow. I promise. I do think he could possibly be the one, but I want to have a good foundation, you know? Like... So many of my friends are just about the physical first, and to me, that's important, of course, but not as important as finding out if he has the same values and morals that I do."

Her comments made Shannon smile inside. She hadn't been sure that Emma had been catching her teaching growing up and especially since the divorce.

"Honestly, I think the divorce shaped my thoughts more than anything else. After all, you had no idea that Dad was going to do what he did, and I don't know that there's any way that you could have prevented it."

"Me either," she said, and she knew there was sadness in her voice. She wouldn't have married her husband had she known that he was going to think it was okay to run off with another woman at any point.

"So I guess I just want to know that Brian doesn't think that divorce is an option. That keeping his word is the most important thing, that when he gets married, it's for a lifetime, not just for now until you find someone better, you know?"

It was obvious that Emma had been deeply affected by the divorce, but it was also obvious that she had taken the teaching that Shannon had given her in her early years and used it to try to find positive lessons in it. She could have focused on the devastation, how she was now a product of a broken home, how her parents weren't together anymore, how her life had changed and not for the better, how she now had to try to somehow assimilate her dad's girlfriend into her life, but Emma seemed to be focused on the positive lessons that she could use in her own life. It was impressive, and Shannon felt proud that she was her daughter.

Emma went on about her work and the things that she was doing and how she was not really using her college degree, although it had been a prerequisite to get hired.

They stepped onto the main street and started walking toward the lake.

"I want to show you the healing garden. That's definitely a new development since we were here, and it's just absolutely beautiful."

"You know, Mom, you never really talked about this place after we left. Was it something to do with Dad? Were there things going on with you two that I didn't see or know?"

That was a good question. Shannon had often wondered if she had missed signs.

"I didn't talk about it because of your sister. That was hard for me. I still haven't gone to her grave."

"You haven't?"

"No. I know, that sounds terrible. But she's not really there. And... Seeing it I guess will just bring back the memories of the funeral and how much I just wanted to leave. I needed to get away. The lake felt dangerous to me, and—"

"And I can understand why. That totally makes sense."

"But it didn't have anything to do with your dad. Or his job. Or anything. I've actually asked myself that a lot, did I miss signs? Was there something there that I didn't see?"

"Yeah. Same. And this move was just kind of shrouded in secrecy and pushed to the side like we couldn't talk about Raspberry Ridge anymore and... After things happened with Dad, it just made me wonder."

"No. It was the way I coped with Yolanda's death. I just needed time in order to face it. You know what they say about time heals all wounds."

"Yeah."

"Well, I guess it didn't really heal the wound, but it made it less painful every time I kind of pulled it out and poked around at it. And finally, after your dad left, I felt like I could get it out and face it and accept the fact—not really accept the fact, but think about Yolanda again. The memories weren't so painful that I couldn't have them anywhere near me, you know?"

"And the lake?" Emma said as they reached the gate of the healing garden and stopped.

"The lake looks beautiful to me. I don't feel even a little bit of malice or anything other than a deep respect for it. I admire the beauty, the grandeur, and the majesty while keeping in mind that like anything else, it could be dangerous. I don't look up at cliffs and think, 'oh boy, it would be dangerous to be on that cliff.' You know?"

"Yeah. Like you don't blame the lake for her death."

"No. I've come to understand that God has a reason for everything, and His timing is perfect, and as much as I don't understand why God would take her, I do understand that there are things that I don't understand, and I might not ever understand until God explains them to me. And that's not just with her death, that's with anything. There's so much I don't know, why would I expect to know everything about why someone might die?"

"That's a good point." Emma took a breath and blew it out. "I love talking to you, because you always show me something I hadn't thought about before, little gems of wisdom, and as I get older, they become more and more pertinent and valuable to me." She laughed a little. "Sometimes I wish I could remember everything that you said to me growing up, because I know I could use it all now. I just don't remember."

"Well, I'm here, just a phone call away, you know that." Emma had a way of making her feel like maybe she did treasure her and find her valuable, even though she was forging her own path.

"You know, Dad said that you seemed relieved about the divorce. Almost like you were escaping something." Emma gazed at her steadily. "I just think you seem sad. Although I also think you are happier than I've seen you in a long time. That doesn't make any sense, does it?"

They laughed together. Before Shannon could say anything, Vera and Dominic came walking down the path toward the gate.

"Oh, I want to introduce you," Shannon said as she saw the figures approaching.

"Okay," Emma said, walking forward as Shannon opened the gate.

"Vera, Dominic, it's so nice to see you. I wanted to introduce you to my daughter, Emma."

"Nice to meet you, Emma," Vera said, holding out her hand.

"I've heard so much about you. It's good to meet you too."

She shook hands with Dominic, and they made a few comments about the garden.

"It's been so good to have your mom around. And she and Lance have really hit it off. It's nice that Lance has finally found a good woman. He's a great guy." They smiled, and then she and Dominic walked off.

Emma waited about four heartbeats before she said, "Lance?" She put a hand on her mom's arm. "You didn't say anything about Lance."

"Oh, he's just a guy that is helping on the repair crew for the inn. I'm not sure why she mentioned him like that. Let me show you around the garden."

She didn't know what she was going to say about Lance. She and Lance didn't really have a relationship exactly. But she definitely had twisted, tangled feelings for him. And she had gone to his house to eat and met his sister.

Thankfully, Emma didn't bring it up again, and Shannon finished the tour of the garden.

As they were leaving, they noticed that Homer and Skyler were in the yard playing with their children. They walked down the sidewalk and stopped at the fence.

Homer and Skyler came over to the fence while their children continued to play, and Shannon introduced Emma to them.

"Nice to meet you. Your mom's been a great addition to the town," Homer said, shaking Emma's hand.

"She sure has. And I know that Lance in particular has enjoyed her company," Skyler said before adding, "It's always great when townspeople get together." Then she mentioned church and the potluck dinner and said that she hoped that Emma was coming.

They chatted for a bit, but didn't stay long, and kept walking up the sidewalk. Shannon wanted to show Emma the store and possibly even the church.

"They mentioned Lance too, Mom," Emma said after they walked a few steps.

"Yeah, I suppose they did," Shannon said. "I don't suppose you remember Fran's store?" she said as she opened the door, the familiar bell jingling overhead as they walked in.

"I remember the smell," Emma said as they walked in.

"Shannon!" Fran said as she looked up and then hurried toward them. "This must be your daughter. She looks just like you."

"You're right. This is Emma. Emma, Fran, she's owned the store for as long as I can remember." That wasn't entirely true. She thought Fran's mother had it when she was little, but definitely Fran had run it for all of Emma's life.

She turned back to the conversation just in time to hear Fran saying, "...and she and Lance have spent a lot of time at the inn. Of course, Dominic and his crew are helping too, but I've heard that your mother and Lance have been doing most of the electrical work themselves."

"Mom? An electrician?" Emma said, looking at her.

"Oh, I didn't mean it like that. She's just with Lance. You know," Fran said, waving her hand in the air.

The conversation went on about the renovations to the inn and how Fran hoped that it brought visitors to the town.

"This must be your daughter," Mertie said as she joined the conversation from several aisles over. "You two share a lot of similarities."

"Well, thanks," Shannon said, and then she introduced the two of them. They chatted for a bit, and Mertie said, "I hope we'll see you at church and the potluck supper. I know Lance and your mom will be there." She smiled and then said, "I need to hurry off."

They bought a couple of coffees and a bag of their favorite chips to enjoy later, and Emma didn't say anything until after they left the store.

"Mother, everyone we meet mentions Lance and you like you're a thing. But you told me that you weren't."

"I don't know that I said we weren't, but we're really not. I guess I've been as surprised as you are," Shannon said, unsure how else to answer that. How did she square the fact that she really did want to be more with Lance, but... "I've just barely been divorced from your dad. It hasn't even been a year since it was final. I mean, I think I've processed most of the baggage that went along with it, although I think some of it will never leave."

"No. I've come to that conclusion too. But another man?"

"There is nothing going on. I promise." She thought about the almost kiss in his truck. If it hadn't been for the tree falling down, she would have kissed him. And she knew she would have enjoyed it.

"So Lance is someone you just met?"

"He and I were together in high school. It was a long time ago." She tried to say it dismissively, but she knew Emma latched onto that.

"You guys had a romance before?"

"We were just high school sweethearts. You had boyfriends in high school. How much do they mean to you now?"

"I look back on them with fondness, true."

"So I guess that's how I look at Lance." She lifted her shoulder and decided that she better be as honest as she could, just in case something actually did happen. "I don't know what's going to happen. But... I don't feel like I'm ready to move on."

Emma let it go, and they didn't talk about it the rest of the afternoon. They made their way back to the inn and sat on the unfinished porch with blankets over their laps, watching the sun go down. The wind had a chill in it that it hadn't had a couple of weeks ago, and the blankets were necessary.

"I'm so glad I was able to visit you," Emma said.

"Me too. And I'm glad you're going to be able to go to church tomorrow. You're going to love it."

"I'm sure I will. There's nothing better than a small-town church. It just always feels so warm and welcoming."

"It really does."

"I think that's what you needed, Mom. This town, this community, Lance maybe? Although, am I gonna get to meet him tomorrow?"

"Yes. I'm sure you'll see Lance tomorrow." Emma seemed to have accepted the fact that Lance might be a part of her life. Although, she thought that maybe Emma thought he was more than what he actually was.

"You seem happy here, Mom. But you also seem...scared almost. Like you're waiting for something bad to happen."

Shannon sat, slowly rocking, realizing that her daughter was probably right. She supposed that after thirty years of thinking that her husband was there, her rock that she could depend on, and then all of a sudden, he just exploded her life with the fact that he was leaving... Why wouldn't she be afraid that another shoe was going to drop at any moment?

"You know, you would always tell me to just trust God. That

whatever He had for you was exactly what you needed. No matter what it was. And that things that looked bad to us weren't necessarily bad things. You don't know how many times I realized you were right about that? When a bad mark on a test just made me study harder for the next one. That losing a friend made me realize areas where I could improve and be a better friend to the next people that came along. That losing a boyfriend was probably the best thing that could have happened because I actually got to see from a distance what kind of person he was. And that he wouldn't have been a good person for me. So many times, you were right. When those catastrophes—those teenage catastrophes—came along."

"I know. You're right. I guess... You know how if you're walking across a bridge and a board breaks underneath you, you're just a little bit more careful when you put your next foot down, right? Because you don't know if another board might break."

"But 'underneath are the everlasting arms,'" Emma quoted softly.

That was a great verse for the bridge example that she had just given. "You're right. God's got me. And I just need to trust Him. No matter what comes."

"I know you do, Mom. I wasn't giving you a hard time, I just—I'm not used to seeing you...okay but not okay, you know?"

"I'm better than I was."

"Right, and you're going to be as good as you were soon. I can't wait to meet this Lance. I feel like he's going to have a hand in your healing."

"I feel like that might be right." And she meant that. Lance really had been good for her. Not only was he a great example, but he seemed to accept her, just as she was, and she knew he was not the kind of person who was going to up and leave at any point. When he said he was going to stay, he meant it. All she had to do was look at Katie to see that.

Fourteen

"It's nice to live in a town where you can walk everywhere," Emma said as they made their way up the main street of Raspberry Ridge toward the church for the potluck supper.

Shannon shifted the Nutella bread that Marina had made for the event. Marina had politely declined when Shannon had asked her if she'd like to go, and that slice of fear that always seemed to hover about her had shown in her eyes for just a moment.

Shannon got the feeling that she'd really like to go, but she was afraid. Afraid of what, Shannon wasn't sure. Maybe that someone would see her and recognize her? Or maybe just afraid of meeting someone who might pull her out of her comfort zone.

She definitely had butterflies of her own. After yesterday, when everyone had been talking about Lance and her like they were some kind of thing, she wasn't sure what to expect today.

But she wanted Emma to really get a feel for what an amazing community Raspberry Ridge was. Not that she thought Emma was going to move there or anything. There were no job prospects, unless Emma wanted to work at the inn or as a clerk at a store or whether she wanted to commute to some other town. But it was a nice idea that

Emma would love the town that she was in, even if she didn't enthusiastically approve of the renovation project.

"In the winter, it might not be so nice."

"You'll just need a pair of cross-country skis," Emma joked, and they both laughed.

Although that might not be a bad idea, Shannon thought to herself. Cross-country skiing would be good exercise.

It had been a long time since she'd been on skis, and cross-country was the best way to go for someone of her age. She wouldn't be going so fast that she might crash into something and break every bone in her body. She was too old to even entertain that idea.

However, she kept that to herself. She didn't need Emma lecturing her about how she shouldn't be on skis at all.

"I hope that Nutella banana bread tastes as good as what it smells. I was hard-pressed not to ask Marina for a sample this morning."

"Same," Shannon admitted.

They hadn't gotten up in time to attend church, which Shannon had been disappointed about, but everyone was invited to the potluck afterward, and Shannon wasn't going to miss it.

"What were you guys gonna do if it rained?" Emma asked as they walked up the drive toward the church which sat on a rise overlooking the lake. It had one of the best views in town, although the view from the church didn't hold a candle to the view from the inn.

"I think everyone just hopes that it doesn't," Shannon said, and then she shrugged her shoulders. "I really don't know. I guess I haven't been here long enough to find out. It's always been nice on potluck days."

This was only the second potluck that she'd attended.

As the tables and congregants came into view, she saw Lance sitting at a table with extra spaces around him, Katie chattering by his side.

When he saw them, he smiled and waved, standing and pointing to the seats that he'd saved for them.

"That must be Lance," Emma said dryly. It was hard to miss how eager he seemed for them to arrive.

"It is," Shannon said, admiring how handsome he was. Not only that, but she thought about his competence as they worked together, how knowledgeable he was, how good he was with his hands, how he treated Katie, and how devoted he was to his family. There was a lot about him to admire. Why did it bother her that the town linked the two of them together? Was it because she didn't want to be linked? Or was it because she didn't know whether he wanted to be?

She wasn't entirely sure.

"Shannon!" Lance said as he hurried over to them. He gripped her in a side hug that lasted maybe a couple of seconds too long. "I missed you this morning, but thanks for sending the text so I didn't worry."

Emma gave her a look.

She hadn't mentioned that she had texted Lance to let him know that she wasn't going to be there. He was expecting her, of course, since they had been sitting together in church. It just made sense, since there was an extra space beside him, and... She didn't know how to excuse herself.

"Here, let me take that," he said, taking the Nutella banana bread from her. "Wow. This smells delicious. Was it you or Marina?" he asked, offering his elbow to Shannon, who took it.

"Marina," Shannon said.

"Mom's helper," Emma said.

"Lance, this is my daughter, Emma. Emma, this is Lance, and that's Katie," she said as Katie hurried up in her distinctive uneven gait.

"Shannon! Lance was so worried about you. He really wants you to eat with us. I hope you're going to sit with us. He told three other people that they couldn't because you were going to."

Katie chattered as she came over and wrapped her arms around Shannon like they were the best of friends.

"Katie, this is my daughter, Emma," Shannon said as Katie stepped back.

"Emma! I'm sure we're gonna be friends. Your mom and my brother like each other a lot. I hope they're going to get married and live with us forever." Katie chattered happily as she wrapped her arms around Emma, who looked a little surprised and then seemed to shrug and just hugged the girl back.

Shannon should have warned Emma about Katie, but she hadn't thought about it. But Emma handled everything with aplomb. It wasn't every day that a person met someone who looked like they were thirty-five but acted like they were ten.

Still, it wasn't like Emma hadn't been out in the world, and she linked her arm with Katie, and soon the two of them were chatting like old friends.

"Come on over," Lance said as he carried the bread to the table where the rest of the food was sitting.

"Marina already sliced it, so it's good to go, all we have to do is kind of unwrap it a little," Shannon said, knowing she was talking to fill space because she was nervous.

"Hey, you're okay. Right?" Lance said, his voice slow, his eyes concerned.

"I'm sorry. I don't know why I'm nervous. I guess I just really want Emma to love Raspberry Ridge as much as I do. I wish we wouldn't have missed church this morning."

"We missed you at the service this morning," Pastor Garnett said as he came up and shook her hand.

"I just said to Lance I wish we wouldn't have missed it."

"I hope everything's okay?" Pastor Garnett said.

"It sure is. I guess Emma and I had a late night last night. Not that we were doing anything, just sitting on the porch talking."

"It was pretty chilly last night, I hope you guys didn't catch a cold or anything." Mertie came up and stood beside Pastor Garnett.

"We had blankets. Probably if we hadn't had blankets, we would have made it to church, because we wouldn't have stayed out nearly as long."

They laughed together, and then Lance guided Shannon over to their seats with a light hand on the middle of her back. It didn't feel dictatorial. It was more of a kind guidance and steadying if she needed it. It felt comforting and warm, and she appreciated it.

With James, she always felt like he was demanding that she do whatever he wanted, and he didn't usually guide her, he led her, dragging her behind him.

She pushed the idea of James out of her head. He had good qualities too. But when she stacked him up against Lance, it always seemed like he was lacking.

As they reached their seats, she noted that Emma had gotten stopped in conversation by Vera, who seemed to be giving her some motherly affection. Skyler then stopped, and she and Katie chatted with Emma in what seemed to be a very animated conversation.

She and Lance had filled their plates and were back eating before Katie and Emma sat down.

"Everyone is so caring and friendly," Emma said as she leaned over the table to confide that to her mother. "You were not lying about the small-town atmosphere. I've never felt so included and seen in my life before."

"It's a pretty great place," Shannon said, but she was smiling hugely inside. This was why she didn't want to miss the church supper.

"But everyone's assuming that you and Lance are a couple." She glanced at Lance, who was chatting with Katie across the table and didn't seem to be paying attention to them. "In fact, someone, I'm not even sure of their name, asked me when you guys were setting a date. Did they mean a wedding?" Emma asked, seriously surprised.

"I don't know..."

"You're stumbling and mumbling around like... It's just funny." Emma laughed and then leaned back. "I'm having such a great time. Someone said there's a guitar and a few other instruments and there might be some dancing later. I wish I would have brought Brian. You should have warned me."

"I'm sorry. There wasn't any dancing last time."

"That's because Wesley and Birdie weren't here. Wesley is a big hockey star, and Birdie is a pop superstar, but they both play and sing as well, and typically when they're around, they treat us to a little bit." Lance nodded over at a couple who had a group of people around them.

As Shannon watched, someone—a little girl—shyly walked up to them and asked for their autograph. It was super cute as the two of them signed their names on her ball cap together.

"They seem just as friendly as the rest of the town," Emma said as she watched them along with Shannon and Lance.

"They're really kind. I've spoken with them some, but their schedules don't allow them to live here full-time. Although both of them are talking about retiring and raising a family here."

"I can't imagine a better place to raise a family," Shannon said, and she wondered why she'd left. She knew why, and she didn't know if she could go back, whether she'd do it differently or not. The deep, searing pain of losing a daughter and being reminded of her at every turn, every step, every view, was a little bit—a lot—hard and intimidating. Maybe she'd needed to get away for a while.

"This Nutella banana bread is amazing," Grace said as she stopped at their table for a moment. She greeted Emma and chatted a bit.

She wasn't the only person who stopped at their table to comment about the Nutella banana bread. It seemed to be the hit of the afternoon.

It was soon gone, and then they had people stopping at their table, asking if Marina would make more so they could try it since it seemed to be legendary already and they didn't even know what it tasted like.

"I think you can include that on the menu for the inn when you open it," Lance said as the fifth or sixth person went by asking for Marina to make it again so they could try it.

"I think Marina got the recipe from Lauren and perhaps tweaked it a bit, and it does seem to have been a big hit. It's crazy what Marina can make out of a little bit of nothing."

"She was definitely a real find," Lance said. "Have you talked to her any more?" he asked, his voice lowering.

Shannon glanced at Emma who was in conversation with Katie. She shook her head. "No. I've offered multiple times to be a confidant, and that's pretty much all I can do. But she's very tight-lipped. She did mention feeling safe here. Which, I understand where she's coming from. The way the town protects its own is endearing, and I know they'll do that for her too."

"Especially after this," Lance said, holding up his last bite of Nutella banana bread. "They'll definitely not want to lose someone who can bake like this."

Shannon laughed. "I'm going to get jealous if you keep talking like that."

Lance's brows rose, and Shannon realized she was flirting, and she shouldn't have been. Especially since she didn't really know how she felt about him.

His voice was lowered and soft as he said, "There's no need. The banana bread is good, but it doesn't hold a candle to you. Not in my eyes."

When did her mouth get dry? Why couldn't she swallow? And her hands felt like they were trembling.

Thankfully, the strains of a guitar being strummed caused everyone to be quiet for just a moment as they all looked around to see what was going on.

"Looks like they're going to play for a while," Emma said, looking eager.

"I wanna dance!" Katie said, clapping her hands.

"You and me both," Emma said, grabbing Katie's hand as a second instrument joined the guitar and someone started to sing.

The girls giggled and got up from the bench, walking to the dance floor, where other people were congregating.

"Emma is so good with her. She treats her like an equal without being condescending. I'm not sure how she does it, but she's a natural with kids."

"She's always been interested in helping people. I kind of thought when she had a major in marketing that maybe she was missing her calling. But she seems to love her job, and I guess that's the important thing." She'd always thought that Emma would end up being a teacher, perhaps even in special education, but when they talked about it, Emma had said that she wanted to get a job where the salary wasn't as limited as what teaching was. Shannon had wanted to tell her that there was more to life than money, but it would have rung a little hollow coming from her, being that while they weren't exactly rich, they were definitely financially well off because of James's job as a corporate lawyer.

They gathered up the garbage that the girls had left behind, along with their own, and walked to the garbage can, being stopped several times by people asking Shannon to make sure that she was okay after she wasn't in church that morning and inquiring about the inn and other things.

By the time they'd gotten back, the guitar had switched to a slower song, and Lance said, "Would you like to dance?"

He looked so hopeful and sweet that she couldn't explain to him that she didn't like to dance in front of people and it would be embarrassing and she might end up stepping on his toes and all the other excuses that she always used in order to not expose herself in public like that.

"Sure," she said instead, just as simple as she could.

The smile on his face made it worth it, and as he led her to the dance floor and wrapped his arms around her, she realized she really didn't care how they looked, it was more about just enjoying the music and the afternoon with someone that she really, truly cared for. Especially since out of the corner of her eye, she could see Emma chatting with some of the townspeople, including Lauren and Claire, who had been good friends of her older sister.

"I wonder if she knew that they were Yolanda's friends," she asked as she nodded in that direction. Lance would know what she meant.

"I don't know. Maybe. She probably remembers more than what you think she does. Maybe she just doesn't talk about it out of respect for your feelings."

"You could be right," Shannon said, trying not to be defensive. After all, it was true that she'd shut down anytime someone tried to talk about Yolanda, at least in the past. "I think coming back here has been as healing as anything could have been. I'm ready to talk about her now."

"Maybe you should let Emma know."

"I think I have. Maybe that's why she feels like it's okay to talk to Yolanda's friends."

Lance nodded, and he moved his hand over her back, just gently, a light caress that was comforting more than anything else.

"Thank you," she said as she looked up at him.

"For?" he asked, looking a little confused.

"For just being amazing. You are...a really great person. And thank you for not holding things against me from way back. Thank you for being my friend now."

Something crossed over his face when she said the word "friend," and she realized maybe he thought that she was trying to put him in his place. She wasn't, not really, but she didn't correct herself. Instead, she just gave herself over to the enjoyment of the beautiful fall day and the perfect weather and the beautiful time that she was having.

Later, as they were walking home, Emma said, "I haven't seen you this happy since I was little. Lance is really good for you, Mom. Don't mess this up by overthinking."

She did have a tendency to overthink. Way overthink.

"I think you're right. I think it's a good idea to just let things happen and make sure that I'm walking the way God wants me to."

Fifteen

Shannon sat at her desk on Monday afternoon organizing paperwork for the inn. She had washed the sheets that Emma had used and allowed herself to be sad for half an hour that her daughter was gone.

It would be a dream come true to have her daughter move to her town, but she knew that wasn't going to happen. So, she could enjoy the visits, deal with the sadness when she left, and then throw herself back into her life, which is what she had done with the paperwork that she knew would be distracting.

Her phone rang as she was going over marketing ideas.

The caller ID showed that it was Julianne, her neighbor in the Detroit suburb when she and James were still married. She hadn't talked to her in more than a year.

"Hello?"

"Shannon, it's Julianne. I used to be your neighbor?"

"Of course. So nice to hear from you."

"It's good to hear your voice too. Although unfortunately, I'm not calling just to chat. I have something I need to tell you."

"Okay?" She felt her stomach drop. Was this going to be more news about her husband? Someone else he had cheated with? She steeled herself to hear.

"I just wanted to let you know that there's been someone walking around town asking about you. And not just you, but the accident with Yolanda. Specific questions. I just thought it was odd."

Shannon froze. Her deepest, darkest fear after losing her daughter. It was the idea that she was responsible. That the authorities just hadn't picked up on the idea that she was to blame. After all, she'd allowed the girls to go out on the lake. And the girls had not been wearing life vests. They should have been. And was it her fault that they hadn't been? She thought she had trained them to do so. She had made them do so anytime she was out on the lake with them, which wasn't that often. She enjoyed looking at it, but being out on it really wasn't her cup of tea.

"I see. What did you tell him?"

"I didn't answer any question that I didn't have to. Any facts that I didn't know I just flat-out told him, any speculation I shut down. But I did think it was important that you knew that something was going on."

"Thank you. I appreciate that."

They talked a little bit more and caught up a bit, but Julianne had to go, and they hung up shortly after.

Shannon felt cold and completely unmoored. Her first instinct was to run. To pack everything up and get out of there. Just disappear somewhere. But she looked around the office—she actually had an office now—and thought about the progress that had been made. About the drywall that had been going up, the electricity that Lance was working on, even as she sat down here. About the crew on the roof—she could hear the hammering in the distance. And the chainsaws that ran in the front yard. By the end of the day, the tree that fell down would be totally cleaned up. By the end of the week, everything that had been broken in the storm would be fixed, plus other strides would be made on the inn. The porch would be finished, and in just a little over a month, she hoped to have the first guest staying.

Did she really want to leave all this? Run away from it?

She already felt like she'd run away twice, from Raspberry Ridge after the accident and then from Detroit after her marriage and family fell apart.

Now, of course, staying in Detroit wasn't appealing at all, but the fact of the matter was, she had run.

She was tired of that. Tired of not facing things. But she really didn't know what to do. She pushed back away from her desk, stumbling a little as she got to her feet.

"Are you okay?" It felt like Marina's voice came from a distance as she stood in the doorway, watching her.

"I'm fine," she said, knowing that was a total and complete lie but wanting Marina to believe her anyway. She didn't know how to tell her that she wasn't fine, that she needed time, that she needed to think, that she had to figure out what to do. The authorities could be coming after her and charging her with…what? Negligence? Homicide? After all, it was her fault her daughter died. All hers.

"I need to leave for a bit," she said to Marina as she stumbled past her, knowing that she was acting oddly but unable to stop herself. She needed to get out of the inn, needed to do something.

She got in her car and started driving with no destination in mind. She ended up driving past the Blueberry Beach high school—she didn't even know how she got there, but she remembered days filled with sun and laughter, snow, and winter games. Snuggling up with hot cocoa around a bonfire, Lance beside her, and her future, endless and exciting in front of them.

She drove past several lake accesses where she had gone boating and swimming with friends, and almost always Lance was part of that. She drove down the road, remembering bringing each of their babies home from the hospital down south where she'd had them before the Blueberry Beach Hospital had been built.. Lance had been a part of everything before James had come into the picture. He had been a part of her life since high school. And she thought he was going to be her future.

She felt like she was in a daze and somehow found herself pulling into the old church, the white one on top of the hill, that her family had gone to faithfully—at least she had, until the day of the accident. It was where Yolanda's funeral had been held and where she was buried.

She parked in the old lot and got out, walking to the familiar spot in the graveyard where Yolanda's grave was. There were flowers there—someone was taking care of it. Probably Claire or Grace or Lauren. It should have been her. If she were a good mother, she would be taking care of her daughter's grave. Maybe the investigator had seen that she hadn't been at the grave, ever, and had realized that it was probably her fault that Yolanda had died.

She stood at the headstone that read, "Beloved daughter and friend, taken too soon."

Shannon fell to her knees, sobbing, as she remembered Yolanda as a baby, the first baby she'd brought home—she'd been scared to death and amazed that the hospital had placed this tiny little human being in her arms and sent her out the doors like somehow she was responsible enough to keep it alive. The struggle to breastfeed, the fear every time Yolanda made a tiny little noise that didn't sound normal. Yolanda's first steps, her first day of kindergarten, her excitement over welcoming a sister and a brother into their home. Yolanda as the big sister, as the responsible one, so many memories. Her beautiful smile, her huge heart, and yes, even her slight rebellion where she insisted that she was big enough to go out with her friends, that her mom shouldn't worry, that she would be fine.

Her desire to be independent, to start stretching her wings. And Shannon's maternal instinct to keep her grounded.

She sobbed, heart-wrenching sobs that came up from her very soul, all the grief that she'd lived with day by day by day, waiting until she was strong enough to feel it or until time had healed enough that she could face the grief.

Even as she cried, she was amazed that it didn't hurt quite as much as what she thought it would. The memories were bittersweet, true, and slightly painful, but not devastatingly sharp like they had been. In fact, she took a little bit of pleasure in thinking about them, even as she cried.

She felt an arm come around her and looked up to see Lance, caring and concern and questions on his face, but he didn't say anything, didn't ask any questions, and when she leaned into him, his arms came around her, and he held her while she cried.

Sixteen

Shannon fingered the tissue in her hand. After Lance had held her for at least thirty minutes, maybe more like an hour, he'd gently suggested that they go to his house. Katie was visiting a friend, and she had agreed.

The only thing they talked about on the way there was when Shannon had asked him how he found her.

He'd explained that he'd come downstairs looking for her, needing her help with the wiring, and Marina had said that she had seemed like she was upset and then left, gotten in her car and driven away. He'd driven around, looking at all the usual spots and on a whim, as a last resort, had tried the cemetery.

"I suppose if I had looked there first, I wouldn't have found you."

He was right. That's where she ended up, not where she started. But she didn't get into that explanation.

They'd just gone to his house, and he'd parked, going around the car and opening her door and helping her out. He'd put his arm around her as they walked up the steps to his front porch. It was slightly secluded with the rosebush climbing on the trellis. A couple of late-season blooms were still adding color to it, but the leaves were turning, and it was getting ready for winter. Like everything else.

Still, it gave them a little bit of privacy as she sat down, and he walked inside to grab a box of tissues and a couple glasses of tea.

He came back out and sat down on the swing beside her, handing her a tissue and setting the tea on the small table next to the swing.

They sat there like that, her pressed against his side, him quiet.

She was waiting for the questions.

They'd been sitting there, just slowly swinging, gently rocking for about ten minutes before Lance spoke.

"After you left, and I had to stay, to help with my family, I kept waiting for you to come back. I thought with the promise ring, you and I would be closer. And it's true, we did talk a good bit at first, and then... I stopped hearing from you at all, and then you called and told me you'd taken the promise ring off. I looked around at Christmas, thought you'd be back, thought we'd talk. Same way in the spring, after the semester was over. I thought I'd see you. And then I heard that you'd gotten married. It felt like it happened really suddenly. I just... I hadn't let go. The idea that you'd be back."

He was quiet for a bit.

And then he said, "And then you were back. After James finished law school, you had a little one, Yolanda, and you were mom and wife, and I knew that my opportunity was over." He was quiet for a bit, and then he said softly, "I was lonely. Really lonely, because all I had was Katie, and she's great, but she's never going to be a wife, never going to be the mother of my children of course, and I felt a little trapped too. Especially after Dad died."

"I'm sorry," she said softly.

"I'm fine now, but at the time, that was just a really hard time for me."

"I didn't see you around town much."

"No. You were busy with your babies and your kids then, and I avoided you on purpose." He hesitated. "Then there was the accident, both yours and Katie's. I didn't know for sure at first that Katie would never be normal again. But you left, and that was hard, and then the knowledge that I wasn't going to be free after Katie turned eighteen. That I was stuck here forever. I don't even know if I really thought about it as being stuck. I just knew I was lonely and I couldn't leave. I had responsibilities I had to take care of."

He paused for a moment. "That's when Carol moved to town. She came to be with her parents."

Shannon felt her breathing grow shallow. She hadn't heard about Carol. Who was Carol?

"She had leukemia when she was little, and she knew that because of the treatments and the type of leukemia that it was, she probably wouldn't live past forty, if she made it that far. She and I met at church, and we talked and... She wasn't you. I told her about you. She knew about you. And... She wanted to marry me anyway. We didn't have a great love, exactly, we were just companionship for each other." He paused. "She was someone to talk to. Someone to ease the loneliness, to look across the supper table at night, to take care of Katie with me. To talk about my hopes and dreams with."

"Wow," she said softly. She had never thought about Lance like that. He seemed so self-assured, so confident, so capable. He was lonely? He had wanted someone, longed for someone so much that he would marry someone he knew he didn't love, just in order to have companionship?

"I knew that I would probably end up taking care of her, but what difference did it make? I was already taking care of Katie. I knew how to do that. Thankfully, when the cancer came back, it came back with a vengeance, and it didn't last long. She was with us one last summer, and she died about this time of year." He blew out a breath. And the swing creaked back and forth. Shannon didn't say anything, waiting for him to finish. "I noticed her grave up there when I was with you. It's not that far from Yolanda."

She hadn't even noticed. She supposed Carol would have had his last name on her grave, whatever it was.

"She was a beautiful woman. Inside and out. Kindhearted, sweet, and gentle. I guess with Carol, I learned that love isn't necessarily about the butterflies and the lust and the passion and even the romance. It's just being there for someone. Showing up when it's hard. Making the conscious choice to be devoted to the person that you've said vows to, even if your heart wants to be somewhere else. That doesn't matter. When you're married to someone, they're your world. You don't allow yourself to look at anyone else. You just don't." He said that rather forcefully, although his voice was still low, and then he continued. "I loved her. Not with a passionate, worldly kind of love, but with a deep, biblical love that would have kept me devoted to her until I died, if she had lived that long."

"I can see that in you," she said softly. It was one of the main differences between James and Lance. Lance was solid and dependable. He might not be flashy, he might not be showy, he might not be able to win every argument he'd ever entered into, and he might not be quick-witted and determined, but he was steady. He was faithful. He was determined to live his life according to his morals and to not be swayed by anything else. And he was always there for her. Always, no matter what she did. He didn't allow her actions to change his. And that was one of the things she most admired about him.

"But after Carol died, I had decided that I didn't want to do that again. You'd left twice. The second time wasn't as hard as the first because I hadn't even allowed myself to look at you. You were married, you had a family. But I'd lost Katie, for all intents and purposes, my dad, my mom, and you twice, and then Carol. I guess I'd kind of given up on the idea that love could come to stay. I still don't know for sure that even being with you is a good idea. But I do know that when you walked into my store, it was like I woke up from a long sleep, and I felt the same unseen thing pulling me toward you, like I'd always felt every time I was in your presence." He paused for just a moment, and then his fingers traced her shoulder lightly as he shifted toward her ever so much. "Shannon, I don't need to know everything right now, but I need to know, are you planning on running again? Because I don't think I can go through losing you again."

He was silent for a while, and Shannon ran over everything that he said. He was a better man than she'd even dreamed. But she didn't want to make promises that she couldn't keep.

"I can't promise I'm not gonna run. I don't want to though. I want to stay here and put down roots. But it wouldn't be fair of me to make promises right now."

He nodded slowly, and she hated that she couldn't give him more. Give him the reassurance that he wanted. She wanted to be able to say that she was staying forever, but she remembered her panic that morning when Julianne had called, and she had talked herself through it and had determined to face whatever she needed to, but would it be fair to drag Lance into that?

If they found her liable for Yolanda's death, she could be dragged away through no fault of her own, through no desire of her own, and she would be leaving Lance, and then he would be stuck, trying to be faithful to someone who was in prison. That wasn't fair to him either.

"Can we just go day by day for now? I know that's not what you want, but... I think that's all I can do right now." It was hard to say those words, hard not to be able to tell him that she was fully committed no matter what, but there were things that were out of her control and things so terrifying to her that she couldn't even say them out loud, not even to Lance.

"I guess that's the other thing I learned, especially with Carol, and Katie too. I can't control everything. I can only control me. And I know that I'm here and I'm not going anywhere."

Seventeen

For the next several weeks, Shannon threw herself into planning for the inn, eventually landing on a soft opening scheduled for the beginning of November. The project was a welcome distraction from her internal turmoil, and it allowed her to focus on the future rather than dwelling on the past.

She had several planning sessions with Marina, where they worked on menu planning, room layouts, and service procedures. Marina was amazing as she suggested seasonal menus and presentation items that could put them on northern Michigan's culinary map.

Shannon had to admit that she had put a wall up between Lance and her, but they still worked together, and they did discuss several times how amazing Marina was and how blessed Shannon was to have her there. There had to be something in her past that gave a clue as to why she was so amazing, but Shannon did not try to probe, and Lance supported that decision. He was naturally included in all the planning, even going with her to different discussions that she had with the community members.

Lauren from the bakery offered to provide breakfast pastries every day, even volunteering to deliver them. She gave them a huge discount in return for having a sign that directed guests to her business on Main Street for more information and for orders, along with her website and contact info. Shannon was more than happy to agree to that. She loved being able to support the local businesses. That was part of her dream when she wanted to open the inn to begin with.

Becky and Rodney were going to advertise their horse and carriage tours and have special tours just for guests, along with a special rate and discount. They also would be advertised in the lobby, as well as each room.

Hobart and his wife were offering fishing excursions on a limited basis. The idea of having a chartered fishing business was something that both of them had been tossing around for a while, and after their meeting with Shannon, they had decided to open that business.

It seemed like the whole town was investing in Shannon's success. With her advertising and everyone else's advertising bringing people into their businesses and having them stay at the inn, it was a win-win situation for everyone.

Grace Gillette, who had been friends with Yolanda, had been helping her with an online presence and the booking systems that she needed. Shannon had had a wonderful conversation with Grace about how she and Trevor had built their woodworking business from nothing, and after speaking with Grace, Shannon's entrepreneurial dreams had soared. It felt like anything was possible. And then came the day she had been waiting for.

She was working with Lance upstairs in the rooms they had rewired just weeks before. Almost everything else was done. There were still a few odds and ends that needed to be finished, but things were coming together beautifully.

She and Lance had developed a rapport between them. It wasn't exactly romantic, but it was a little more than friendship. He had respected what she had said about needing time and not being sure of what she was doing, and he had backed off and given her the space that she needed in order to come to grips with herself.

She didn't know whether she was any closer to that happening or not, but she appreciated him not withdrawing his presence and friendship from her. It was something that she'd leaned on during these difficult days—difficult but exciting days—as she threw herself into the inn project.

"One more room completely ready with drywall and ready for the last coat of paint. Then we can put the appliances in and you're going to have another floor that's ready for guests."

She was just about ready to open her mouth and say that she didn't have any guests booked, when her phone dinged.

It was an odd sound, one she hadn't heard before, and she tried to remember why it sounded familiar. And then as she brought the phone up to look at it, she knew.

"Someone booked!" she said, jumping up and swiping quickly on her phone.

"It's a couple! They booked the whole weekend, both Friday and Saturday nights!" She gasped, putting her hand over her mouth and looking at Lance, who looked almost as excited as she felt.

"It started! We did it! Our first guests!" She jumped up and down, putting her arms up and then grabbing Lance and swinging around.

He put his arms around her and lifted her up, smiling up into her beaming face. "That's awesome. I am so thrilled for you. What date?"

"Opening weekend!" she said, glancing at her phone again. "I can't believe it!" In her excitement, she barely realized that he was holding her tight against him, her feet off the floor, their bodies pressed together.

Then, as he stopped spinning her and slowly allowed her to slide back down to the floor, her hands just naturally came to rest on his shoulders, and the smile that had been on her face froze as she stared into his eyes.

"This is a dream come true," she said as she looked up at him.

He nodded. "It sure is. And you're beautiful when you see your dreams come true."

She wasn't sure whether he lowered his head or whether she stood up on tiptoe, but whatever it was, they started moving toward each other until a sound in the hall made her jerk back.

"Did I hear that we have our first guests?" Dominic said before he appeared in the room.

She'd already jerked back, and if he noticed the awkward feeling between Lance and her, he didn't let on. He was followed into the room by several other workers whom she'd gotten to know by name over the time that they'd spent at the inn, and pretty soon, everyone was high-fiving everyone else, and the moment between Lance and her was just a memory.

A sweet, beautiful, warm memory that she would cherish forever. Even if they hadn't kissed, it was a celebration between the two of them. He had supported her every step of the way, and she had leaned on him, and they had gotten the news together. It couldn't have panned out more beautifully if she had planned it.

There was excitement in the air the rest of the afternoon, and several people from town were so thrilled they stopped in. The whole town was buzzing about their first booking, and Marina even made a cake in celebration, so they had refreshments to offer their guests as well as excitement.

By the time everyone left, and it was just Lance and her standing on the freshly built and beautifully restored front porch, it felt perfectly natural for them to hold hands as they watched the sunset.

She wasn't sure whether his fingers entwined with hers first, or whether she had reached out to him, but it felt like a perfect and a fitting end to the day.

"You did it. These dreams, these things that no one was sure that you could do, are finally happening."

"I couldn't have done it without you. Every step of the way, I felt your strength behind me. And when that failed, you pointed me to the Lord and told me He had something planned for me. I can't believe it."

They gave each other soft smiles and then looked back out at the sunset. There were a few things in her life she needed to work on, things she needed to get right, and her relationship with Lance was one of them, but for now, the inn planning had taken over it all, and to see it come to fruition was a success that gave her a satisfaction that she couldn't put into words. And to share it with Lance made it perfect.

"Thank you. You are the best." Her tone was soft and sweet, and his eyes glowed as he looked down at her. If he thought about kissing her, she couldn't tell. But she definitely thought about it. Thought about the earlier almost kiss and how she wanted their relationship to move in that direction as well. But maybe just one thing at a time. They were building something here, something like the inn, and they couldn't rush it. It had to happen and unfold the way it was supposed to, without her rushing into things.

Eighteen

Two weeks before the inn's official opening, Shannon stood in the inn's lobby arranging flowers. There were still workmen wandering around at times and a few things that needed to be finished —mostly fixtures that needed to be hung and things that were backordered. She couldn't believe how quickly everything came together and how amazing the old inn looked, restored to its former grandeur. She had to admit she was excited about the future.

She was a little sad though, since Lance no longer had an excuse to show up every day. Most of his work was finished, although Dominic had pretty much assigned all the odds and ends to Lance to finish up.

Still, she missed him. Missed working with him. Missed having him around.

She was deep in thought, not even really paying attention to the bouquet of flowers that she was arranging, when a man in an expensive suit walked through the front door.

She turned, taking him in, realizing that everything about him screamed that he was not local, and her instincts said even more loudly that he was dangerous.

"Hello, I'm looking for Shannon," he said, then paused as if trying to remember her last name.

"I'm Shannon Callahan. That was my married name," she said evenly, trying to hide the fact that she was afraid. She clasped her hands behind herself so that he would not see they were trembling.

"I'm Detective Rick Morison." He grabbed a badge out of his pocket, flipped it around, then put it away before she could actually read what was on it. "I have questions about the incident that happened years ago in which your daughter drowned."

"All right," she said, closing her eyes and steeling herself. That seemed like it would be a normal reaction anyway and not one born out of total fear and nervousness that some type of official person was standing in front of her, and she was scared to death she was going to be charged with murder.

"What happened that day?"

"My daughter and her friends went out on the lake. From what I understand from them, a rogue wave flipped the kayak over, and Yolanda never resurfaced. They were in a hurry to get back to shore because there was a storm coming, and they looked for her for a while, couldn't find her, and came back."

"And where were you?"

"I was home."

"Why weren't you out there with them, supervising?"

"They were all experienced on the lake. It was supposed to be a nice day. There were no thunderstorms forecast." She said that all robotically. She had answered those questions a hundred times in her head and almost as many to the authorities when they came to question her. They hadn't spent a whole lot of time with her, since they had seen that she was a grieving mom and knew that she certainly hadn't caused the accident. Whether she was going to be charged with negligence or some other associated crime had always been her fear.

"What else can you tell me?" the man asked, and she shook her head.

"I was grief-stricken. Absolutely devastated that my daughter might be gone. I really don't remember a whole lot about the investigation or about what happened. I'm not a good person to talk to about those details."

She lifted a shoulder and then looked him in the eye. "The police have a full record. I suggest you contact them if you're interested in what all of the witnesses said about that day."

Morison smiled, but it did not reach his eyes as he handed her his card. "You can contact me if you think of anything else."

Out of the corner of her eye, Shannon could see Marina come to the door of the kitchen and push it open. She froze when she saw the official-looking man in the suit and then slowly backed away, closing the door until it was only open a crack.

After Morison left and the front door clicked closed behind him, Marina hurried out.

"I know that type. That man is dangerous. What did he want?"

"He claimed to be a detective asking questions about the accident in which my daughter drowned."

"I'm so sorry. That must be hard. Did it happen a long time ago?"

Shannon filled Marina in on a few of the overarching facts. She didn't go into detail, because she was more shaken than she cared to admit.

"Who do you think he really was? Do you really think he was a legitimate detective?"

"I don't know. I really don't. I have no experience with this type of thing. My ex-husband is a lawyer, it's true, but he typically works for corporations. It's not usually this type of case that he takes on."

Marina nodded. "I think whatever that man wants, it's not about justice. It's about money or revenge. He didn't look legit to me at all. He actually looked like he was planning on hurting someone or like he was hunting prey. Did you see his eyes?"

"I did. They looked a little soulless," Shannon said, suppressing a shiver at the memory.

They talked a little bit, and then each of them went back to their tasks, although Shannon had a hard time focusing on the flowers. She couldn't think about them and ended up standing, staring into space. That's where she was when Lance rushed in forty-five minutes later.

"Are you okay?" Lance asked as he strode across the floor immediately, coming to her side and putting his arm around her.

She leaned into his side, drawing strength from his warmth and his confidence.

"I am feeling better now," she said honestly.

"You're trembling. Let's sit down."

He led her to a chair, one of the few that were grouped around the lobby, cozy and intimate in their setting, and he sat down in a chair that was angled toward her, his knee touching hers, his hand holding hers.

"What did he want?"

She shook her head. "He was asking pointed questions about the accident that killed my daughter, but I don't think that's what he really wanted. Or he wasn't trying to find out facts. He's trying to hurt someone, I think." She remembered what Marina had said, and she shivered. She didn't have as much experience as Marina probably did, but she still got a terrible vibe and an even worse feeling from even thinking about the man.

The front door opened, and Shannon couldn't stop her gasp and fearful gaze. She sighed with relief when she saw it was just Homer, looking around, appreciating the view, and then his eyes landed on her.

His gaze firmed up, and he strode over.

"Looks pretty nice in here," he said. "It's been a bit since I was in and saw it."

"Thanks. It's all come together really well. We just have a few little odds and ends to finish up. Opening is in two weeks."

"That's exciting. The whole town's buzzing about it." He paused, glanced at where Lance clasped her hand, and then gave Lance a serious look. "The town is also buzzing about the man who visited you today." His gaze went back to Shannon. "I have a little bit of experience in tech. A lot, I guess. It's my job. I just wanted to offer to look the guy up if you wanted me to."

Shannon glanced at Lance, who nodded.

She dug the card that Morison had given her out of her pocket. "His name is Rick Morison. And this is the card he gave me. That's all the information I have on him. He flashed a badge, but it was too fast for me to actually read anything it said. I don't think he was an official government person. I think he was maybe a PI or something?"

Homer nodded. "This is not my area of expertise, although if there's information on him on the internet, I can find it. I'll have to leave it up to someone else to make sense of the info."

"I appreciate you offering," Shannon said.

"Me too. I don't have a good feeling about this," Lance said, and it surprised Shannon. He hadn't mentioned that to her. Maybe he hadn't wanted to scare her.

"I don't know a whole lot, but do you have someone staying here with you at least for this evening? I don't think he's the kind of guy who's going to kill you in your bed or anything, but I definitely would want to have someone with me if he shows up again."

"I was planning on staying. Katie and I can come and spend the evening here," Lance said, and Homer nodded.

"That will make my wife feel a lot better, and me too. Just let me know if you need someone to take your place. I feel like you'll be safe at night, especially since the security system has been installed, but I definitely think that someone should be with you during the day."

"I'll take care of it. Thank you," Lance said, standing up and shaking Homer's hand.

True to his word, Lance left only to pick up Katie and to bring her back for supper. Marina had made enough for everyone, and it was delicious as always.

Lance and Katie stayed until eleven o'clock, when Katie could barely keep her eyes open. He obviously did not want to leave, but Shannon and Marina insisted that he take Katie home to bed.

He said that he would be back to drive around the inn a few times at night, and if he saw anything odd, he'd be in. He knew the code to the door, and they felt like everything would be fine as long as they stayed inside.

But neither one of them felt like going to bed, so they sat beside the newly restored fireplace with an herbal tea blend that Marina had brewed in order to relax them both.

The stress of Morison's visit had them both on edge, and maybe that was why Marina began to talk.

"That man reminded me of the investigators my ex-husband used to threaten me with."

Shannon's eyes widened, and she lifted her brows at Marina, silently urging her to go on.

Marina ran a finger over the edge of her teacup. "I was married to

Vincent Castellano, heir to a restaurant empire in upstate New York. He was abusive. He was brilliant in the kitchen, a culinary genius, still is, but behind closed doors, he beat me mercilessly."

Shannon gasped. Her hand went to her throat. "Poor thing."

Marina acknowledged her words and then continued. "I put up with his psychological and physical abuse. He isolated me from family and friends, and he had my every move monitored. He owned restaurants from New York to Chicago, and he is well-regarded in the circles. As rightly he should be. He does have a talent in that area. But unfortunately, there was nowhere I could work in the industry without him finding me. So no matter how badly I might have wanted to escape, I didn't know what I would do to support myself after I did. Thankfully, we had no children."

"My goodness," Shannon said.

"I ran away several times, and he always brought me back. The beatings were worse then. I decided that I had to run away one last time and make it so that it lasted forever." She took a wobbly breath. "I faked my own death. I must have done a pretty good job, because I haven't heard from him, but there has been someone calling me. I don't know who he is, but I'm scared. Scared that whoever has been calling will tell my ex. That he'll send someone like Morison to get me." She sighed. "I've been legally dead for eight months. I staged a boating accident, and I almost did drown swimming to shore. But it must have been convincing enough because I did catch a little bit on the news that they had a funeral for me."

Shannon realized she wasn't the only one who was running from her past. But Marina had a legitimate reason to do so. She, on the other hand, was just trying to get away from her guilt and her grief. Or maybe she just needed to put time between them. That's what she kept telling herself. Wasn't that a legitimate coping mechanism? But for how long did she want to do it? Was she ready to stand and face it?

"So...that man was asking about your daughter?" Marina held her tea, stirring it gently and giving Shannon as much time as she needed to formulate her thoughts. After Marina had confided in her, she couldn't do anything except trust her in return.

"He was asking me about my daughter's death. I was in charge of the girls the day she died. They asked my permission to go boating on the lake, and I gave it to them. Of course, I told them to wear life jackets, and I learned later that they did not. A rogue wave capsized the boat after they saw that there was a storm coming in. They were in a hurry to get to shore, but they realized that Yolanda never came up after the boat turned over. None of the girls ever saw her surface again. It's odd, because Yolanda was such a good swimmer." She shook herself. "Anyway. I've had the guilt, along with the sharp grief of losing my daughter, ever since that day that it was my fault. I'm the one who gave them permission. If I had just said no. If I had gone with them. If I would have had someone watch the younger kids so that I could have been there somehow. I don't know. I guess I just feel like I need to stop questioning it and accept the fact that what happened happened. And I thought I was almost to that point. That God allowed it for a reason. That I had things I needed to learn. Other people did too. And that Yolanda is in heaven with Him, much happier than she would be on earth. As hard as it is to face, it's true. But with Morison's arrival, he's brought back all the guilty feelings, all the reasons that I blame myself. And I've never admitted that to anyone. The grief is normal, but the guilt... I don't know if people would understand, and if I said it, maybe they would think that I was right. I should feel guilty because it was my fault." She put a hand on top of Marina's. "I know our stories are not exactly similar, but it's the idea that we have to face it sometime. And that having a town like this behind us makes it easier."

"Yes. I agree. I don't want to pretend to be dead for the rest of my life. Scared to use any kind of electronic payment method or anything that Vincent might find me through or be able to track me down. Living with fear is terrible. Living with guilt is even worse. And running might be the answer temporarily, but running never is permanent."

They nodded at each other, both of them thinking about their past and about how they were going to face the future. It seemed like as the fire burned low, and the night deepened around them, that a friendship was forged that would last for the rest of their lives, no matter what happened with their past, their present, or their future.

The next morning, Shannon woke feeling lighter than she had in years. Was that what having a deep, heart-to-heart talk did? She had finally admitted the guilt that she felt and the fear as well.

She hoped Marina felt just as good when she woke up. But it was Marina's day off, and she was nowhere to be seen, so Shannon decided that she would walk to the general store for a cup of coffee and to just chat with Fran for a little bit. She just felt that good.

It was only a ten-minute walk, and while the wind was chilly, she bundled up tight, and it felt invigorating rather than cold.

Unfortunately, her feel-good mood was short-lived when she saw Morison's rental car parked outside the general store.

Call her a coward, but she waited until the investigator had left before she walked in. Even the cheerful bell ringing above her head didn't dispel the black mood that had fallen upon her.

"Shannon, darling. How are you?" Fran said, bustling to her like a mother hen and gathering her in her arms like a hen might gather her chick to her.

Shannon laid her head on Fran's shoulder and allowed herself to be comforted. "I was doing good until I saw Morison was here. What did he want?"

"Oh, he's asking about you. About the accident and whether your actions after the accident were because of guilt rather than grief."

Shannon's heart froze.

Fran waved her hand. "I didn't answer him more than what I absolutely had to. I know that's what everyone else has been doing, since he's been systematically visiting everyone in town, asking his silly questions and probing where he doesn't need to and where it's none of his business anyway."

"I guess in a way I'm glad for it. It's brought some things out into the open that I've been clutching pretty close."

"Really?" Fran asked, lifting her head and stepping back a little from Shannon.

Shannon nodded.

"I think you'll talk about this better over a cup of coffee," Fran said with a little bit of her old fire and humor coming back.

"I think you're right."

Shannon followed her to the counter where Fran poured a cup of coffee into a to-go container and doctored it up just the way Shannon liked it.

Shannon pulled her wallet out, but Fran shook her head. "It's on the house. I've already gotten more business in the store because of the inn going up. I should be paying you every time you set foot in here."

Shannon smiled and murmured her thanks before she took a sip of the warm, rich brew.

"I've clutched my guilt close to me all of these years. I wonder, sometimes, if I had said no, if I had gone with them, if I had found someone to watch the kids—all the things that you question yourself about, I think, naturally after a tragedy like this. But I just couldn't let the stuff go. Like it was my fault. I was able to talk to Marina about it yesterday, and I just feel so much better. I don't know where this guy's investigation is going to go, but I do know that he made me face some things that I didn't want to face and open up about things that I hadn't been able to talk about before. So I suppose I have to thank him in a way."

"Maybe you should," Fran said with a little laugh. "But I'm not going to. And I don't think anyone else in town is going to either. We're all kind of circling the wagons around you, and if he wants information, he can just go find it at the police station like everybody else does. We don't need our lives uprooted or probed or disturbed just because he's got a bug in his bonnet somehow."

Shannon smiled and enjoyed the feeling that came over her as she realized that the entire town was on her side. "I think I'll go see Lance. I don't really need anything at the hardware store, but I think I'd like to talk to him."

"I know he'd like to talk to you," Fran said with a wink. "You've led that poor boy on a merry chase, but that's another thing you'll want to get settled from your past. In my opinion, you never should have left without settling things with him in the first place, and just between you and me, that loser you married didn't deserve you."

"I know you're right. I never should have taken his promise ring off. I've regretted that decision all of my life. And you're also right that James doesn't hold a candle to Lance. He's a good man. In fact, he might be a little too good for me."

"Now don't you go telling yourself that. You two are the perfect match."

She said goodbye to Fran and walked out the door, wanting to whistle she felt so good.

Her mood was dampened a bit as she saw Morison walk out of the hardware store.

But she knew that Lance, of all the people in the town, would protect her and defend her to his dying breath, so she didn't worry too much. Not that she had anything else to hide. Not really. Nothing except her feelings for Lance. And maybe that was the reason she wanted to go to the hardware store all of a sudden. She needed to get those out in the open as well. So what if she admitted that she was madly, crazily in love with him and wanted to spend the rest of her life with him, and he wasn't sure he was ready for that yet? So what? At least he would know where she stood.

The atmosphere as she walked into the hardware store was not what she had anticipated, though. And after taking one look at Lance's face, she knew that she wouldn't be confessing her feelings anytime soon.

"Lance?"

"Shannon. That dude was here asking about you."

"I figured. I saw him leave. Are you okay?"

Lance pushed out a sigh and then ran both hands through his hair, turning away from her. It was the turning away that made her heart freeze.

"Lance?" she asked, wanting to step forward and touch him, but something held her back.

He ripped his hands from the sides of his head and threw them down beside him as he turned around. For the first time since she'd known him, it looked like he was angry.

"Shannon, I feel like I've been patient. More patient than a man ever would be expected to be. Probably more patient than anyone could be. And yet I get blindsided by this dude who's asking questions about you, and I feel like I don't know you at all. I feel like I'm standing here by myself, and every time I try to get close to you, you pull away. You move back, you shut me out. How much do I have to take before you let me in?"

She wasn't quite sure what the conversation could have been about, but maybe it wasn't about anything different than anyone else had talked about. It just brought to the surface all the feelings that he had. And maybe this had to do with her leaving him before.

"You just need to talk to me," he said.

She wasn't quite sure what it was, whether it was his anger, or the unfair accusations, or the worry that the one person in her life who had been a constant, who had always seen her for what she was and loved her anyway, was slipping away from her, but she reacted with anger.

"Maybe this is why I left this town in the first place. Small towns where everyone thinks they're entitled to know your business. Maybe we're both fooling ourselves about the idea of you and me ever working." Maybe it was her fear that she would actually be alone after all. Or maybe it was the idea that if she was going to destroy something, she wanted to do it in the best way possible, but words that she never intended to say, and really didn't mean, left her mouth. "You never left this place, never grew beyond taking care of other people. Maybe I need someone who understands the real world."

She could see the hurt on his face. See that the half-truth she spoke had hit the mark. That he really hadn't ever left the town, and maybe that was something that he regretted or at least wished had been different.

Shannon knew before she turned on her heel and stomped out of the hardware store that she had made a terrible mistake, but she didn't want to admit it. It was her pride more than her fear that kept her from running back in and apologizing. She wished she could get herself to turn around, but she stormed all the way home to the inn and into her bedroom, closing the door with a quiet click before she threw herself on the bed and sobbed into her pillow. It was a teenage thing to do, and it didn't really make her feel better, and she knew that it wasn't going to solve anything, but it was all she could do.

Twenty

Shannon hadn't figured out how she was going to apologize by the time evening came.

Marina had popped her head into her room, asked if she needed anything, and then said she was going for a drive.

She didn't even have a friend to talk to.

Around six, Shannon figured that it was about time for her to get up and do something. Maybe she could make it to the door and head out to see Lance. Or even better, maybe he would come to see her.

But she hardly thought so. She was the one who had hurled all the insults and stormed out.

She didn't mean any of them. She didn't even know why she said them, other than sometimes when a person was upset, they said things they didn't mean. She thought she was over that.

"Knock knock?" a voice called from the kitchen doorway before the door pushed open, and Skyler appeared, holding a kettle. "Homer told me Lance looked like someone died, and you look about the same. Do you want to tell me what happened?"

She appreciated having a familiar, friendly face. "Want to come on in? That smells delicious."

"Chicken noodle soup. Easy to make, and good for more than the common cold," Skyler said with a smile. She took a breath and looked at Shannon with some trepidation. "I hope you don't mind, but Vera called an emergency Bible study, and the location is here."

That made Shannon smile. Her friends were coming. They knew she had a rough go of it, and they were coming to support her.

"Of course it's okay. And thankfully, the place is clean and ready for visitors. And friends. Especially friends."

Skyler set the soup on the table and walked around to give Shannon a hug. "I think we've all gone through hard times, but it seems like you've had it worse than others."

"I don't think I have it any worse, and a lot of it is because of my own doing. I can trace every problem I have back to my own poor decisions." Except for Yolanda's death. That really wasn't her fault, was it? She was still working on that one.

As each woman arrived, they set their food down and gave Shannon a gentle but firm hug and some comforting words.

Soon they were all seated at the table, enjoying the food.

"I've just made some terrible mistakes," Shannon found herself saying during a lull in the conversation. No one had directly questioned her or accused her of anything. But somehow she found out that there had been a few witnesses to the words that she and Lance had exchanged in the hardware store. One of the benefits—or one of the drawbacks— of small towns was that there was probably going to be a witness for pretty much anything.

"Honey, I've watched you these past months. You are not the same person who ran away at eighteen, going to college, choosing to spread your wings and fly when maybe you weren't quite ready, and then who left again after the accident. You're stronger now. Your faith in God is bigger and deeper, and your ability to look at others and see what you can do for them is immeasurable. Look at this inn." Vera moved a hand around, indicating the beautifully restored kitchen they were sitting in. "Unfortunately, I think at times you're still letting fear drive the car."

It was a gentle reminder that what she had said to Lance wasn't true. It came from a place of guilt, but more than that, fear.

"I think you're right. I think the idea that a man could be faithful, that I could trust him, that he would be there for me... My ex just wasn't. He was all about himself. I think back on our marriage, and every time we had a disagreement, it was me going to him. It was always me trying to make our house a home, trying to create a family atmosphere. He would have been content to walk away from me twenty-nine years ago. But I was the one that held it all together. And I guess the idea that a man can see me for me, and all my mistakes and all my failures, and all the times that I let him down, and still love me... It scares me. It's like it's too good to be true."

"The thing about our fear is that when we bring it to light, when we face the thing that we're so afraid of, oftentimes we realize that it really wasn't as big and bad as what we thought it was. And I'm not talking about your fear, I'm talking about my own." Mertie spoke from the head of the table. "I just know that's how it worked for me. Once I brought things out into the open, it really didn't seem so bad at all."

They spoke a little more, but Shannon felt relief that her friends not only were supporting her but had gone through similar things. She knew that; she just needed the extra nudge that they were giving her.

Eventually, they finished eating and moved to the sitting area in front of the fireplace, where they all gathered in cozy chairs and soon had a crackling fire with tea and coffee and hot chocolate on a little stand in their midst.

There weren't too many things that hot chocolate couldn't help, Shannon thought to herself as conversation floated around them. Eventually, the ladies started talking about the detective who had been there.

"He pretty much stopped everyone and spoke to us all. And the entire town's response was unified resistance. Fran refused to serve him at the store," Grace said with a laugh.

Mertie smiled. "My husband just hasn't been able to find time to meet with him," she said with a wink. Everyone knew that Pastor Garnett would drop anything to be with any of the townspeople, so the fact that he hadn't been able to find time made everyone giggle.

"I know Dominic's crew has been making his life exceptionally uncomfortable. Anytime he stops in to try to talk to them, accidents seem to happen all around him." Vera winked at the ladies. "I heard someone accidentally dropped a hammer on his toe."

The ladies laughed again, and Shannon felt surrounded by warmth and love and accepted for exactly who she was.

As the evening drew to a close, Vera closed the meeting with prayer, and every woman took their turn, praying for courage for Shannon and healing between her and Lance. Every woman showed faith that it would happen, that Shannon would do the right thing, and that Lance would forgive her. That their relationship would be blessed and move in the direction that the Lord wanted it to.

Shannon hoped in her heart that the Lord had reconciliation in mind and a long, beautiful future between Lance and her.

After all, He'd given her the inn, but what good was that without someone to share it with?

Twenty-One

It took a couple of days for Shannon to be able to get away. There was so much going on at the inn with her first guests expected to arrive soon and other guests already booking.

So, it was Saturday morning before Shannon was able to walk to town with the intent of seeing Lance.

She kept her coat bundled around her, although the sun was warm on her face. Soon snow would be flying and winter, her favorite season, would be descending in full force.

She made it to the main street and turned right to head to the hardware store and saw Katie out in the yard, raking leaves.

She took in a deep breath and smiled when Katie saw her, squealed, dropped the rake, and ran to the fence, throwing her arms around Shannon and giving her a huge hug.

She missed Katie, even though it had only been a couple of days. The idea of never seeing her again or of just being a distant friend tugged at her heart. She had hoped to be family.

Katie stepped back and said, "Shannon, why aren't you and Lance friends anymore? He's sad all the time." She tilted her head. "You look sad too."

Katie's observation was innocent and direct, just the way Katie was.

Shannon took a breath. She wasn't sure if she would be able to explain in terms that Katie could grasp. "Sometimes relationships are complicated. Sometimes people do things that bother us or that hurt us on accident and there's just…"

"I don't understand. If you love each other and you're both sad, why don't you just say you're sorry and be happy again?" Katie made it sound so simple.

Maybe it was that simple.

"I guess that's why I'm here." Maybe she had thought that they would talk about it a little more, but they really didn't need to. Unless he didn't want to hear from her. After all, she was the one who was to blame for everything.

"I'm so glad. Lance stares at the inn all the time. He mopes around the house. He's even been grumpy, and Lance is never grumpy. Especially with me. I'm his princess," Katie said, batting her eyes.

"I know you are. You're precious to him."

"But he's been sad. And I don't like it when he's sad."

"I don't like it when he's sad either. But I don't know if I can do anything to fix it."

"He's making pancakes right now. He sent me outside to rake leaves and to work up an appetite. He always makes too many, and he said maybe if I had a better appetite there wouldn't be any left over. But now that you're here, you can have some. I didn't work up an appetite anyway," Katie said, looking back at the pitiful pile of leaves she'd managed to get together.

"I don't want to intrude on your Saturday morning breakfast."

"Lance wants you here. I know he does. And if he doesn't, I'll just say that you're my friend and you're having breakfast because I invited you."

"You're really sweet, Katie," Shannon said, wishing that she could be just as innocent and happy and simple as Katie was. If only life were that simple. She had a feeling that Lance was going to require more than an apology from her, but maybe Katie was right. Maybe that was all she needed. The idea that Lance was sad was almost funny. Except… What if it was true? Maybe he really did miss her. Maybe he really was upset. If it was true, what did it mean? Did he like her as much as she liked him?

She supposed his words implied that, but she just wasn't sure. It felt like taking a big risk to go in with Katie, but she walked to the gate and unlatched it, and Katie was there as she walked through, slipping her hand into Shannon's arm and walking with her up the sidewalk, chattering all the way.

Before they reached the porch steps, Shannon happened to look up, and she saw Lance standing at the living room window, staring outside at them.

Because of the glare on the glass, she couldn't tell whether he was happy or sad or angry, or what. She could just see his eyes, penetrating across the distance, and felt her own reaction, a combination of fear and excitement and reluctance to move. He made her want to turn around and run away.

"Lance makes good pancakes. They're the best pancakes I've ever eaten. He tells me that someday he'll teach me how to do it, because mine never turn out like his." Katie was still chattering as they walked up the steps and across the porch.

Lance disappeared by the time Katie opened the door and Shannon walked through. Was he running? Maybe he just didn't want his pancakes to burn. Or maybe he didn't want to have to spend any more time with her than what was absolutely necessary.

But then she thought about Katie and her simple directness. Maybe her developmental delay actually gave her clarity that adults lose. Love is simple. Fear is the only thing that makes it complicated. Fear and pride. And Shannon had way more of both of those things than any person should.

As they walked into the kitchen, she saw Lance standing on the other side, not facing the counter, but facing the door, and the look on his face clearly held hope and maybe a little surprise.

"I told you she'd come! Now we can all be happy!" Katie announced as they walked into the kitchen.

Lance looked a little embarrassed at Katie's outburst, and Shannon had to smile. Although she was embarrassed too. Katie shouldn't have known before she did that she was going to come apologize.

"I would have been here sooner, but things are so crazy at the inn right now. I kept getting waylaid every time I tried to get out."

He jerked his head but didn't say anything.

She realized she hadn't said anything at all about why she was trying to come here.

"I said some things that were unkind. A lot of things that were very unkind, and I'm sorry. I did not mean to hurt you. Actually, at the time I probably did, because I was angry and upset and my mouth ran away from me. I have no excuse other than that. I wish I could say it would never happen again, but I guess I can't."

"I guess that happens to everyone. It happens to me too. I'm sorry for getting impatient. You've been through a lot, and I've been telling myself ever since you came back that I just needed to wait and let you work through it, and I didn't do that the last time we spoke. I wanted more from you than you were ready to give."

More? How much more did he want? She was ready to give...a lot. Everything? She wasn't quite sure about that.

"I guess it's hard for me to trust."

"That makes sense. I understand that."

She kind of thought that someone who hadn't been cheated on probably wouldn't understand how difficult it was to trust, but maybe he did. Maybe he had thought about it and could put himself in her shoes and understand how scary it was to put her heart in someone's hands when the last person who had had it had treated it so callously and carelessly.

"I'm hungry," Katie said, sounding impatient and a little whiny. "Can't we eat?"

Shannon smiled, and Lance, after seeing her grin, grinned back.

"We probably should eat while they're still hot. Nothing is worse than a pancake that won't melt the butter on top of it."

"You've never made bad pancakes. But they are better if they're hot," Katie said while she went and got plates and set the table.

Shannon moved to the silverware drawer, which was over by Lance. He stepped out of the way so she could open it.

"It's good to see you," he said low, and she supposed she was the only one who heard it.

She lifted her face to his. "I missed you. I missed you so much, and I still feel terrible."

He shook his head. "We'll talk later."

But his expression said that she didn't need to worry about it. That everything was forgiven.

They chatted lightly over pancakes, with Katie holding up most of the conversation, chattering about the leaves and working in the yard and the things that she had been doing at the places where she stayed and how she was helping some in the hardware store, earning a little bit of money by sweeping the floor every day at closing.

It made Shannon's heart warm to think about how careful and kind Lance had been to Katie. And how sweet and innocent she had stayed, totally secure in the love of the adults around her, and that was almost entirely Lance's doing.

Their easy domesticity felt sweet and warm and cozy and right. Like this could be a real family.

It made Shannon's heart sad to think that it could have been her actual family, with Lance being the father of her children, and Katie a part of their table always as each baby came home from the hospital.

But that wasn't her life, and she couldn't regret the life she'd lived. Otherwise, it would be wasted. She needed to look at the lessons, learn what she could from them, and move on.

After the pancakes had all been eaten with just one left over, and the table cleared and the dishes done, Katie went off to play with some other kids who were outside in their yards also raking leaves into a pile so they could jump into them.

Lance offered his hand to Shannon and asked her if she wanted to sit on the porch swing.

"Maybe it's a little cold for that?" he added.

"I can handle it if you can," she said, although it was chilly out.

"Maybe we should just sit in here on the loveseat. I can start a fire."

"That's cozy," she said. Maybe he took that as her preference, which it was, and he knelt before the fireplace for a little bit until he had a nice healthy flame going.

Shannon, sitting on the loveseat, admired again how competent and good he was with his hands. He built a fire the same way he wired at the inn—with a deliberateness and a competence that drew her and attracted her.

"There. Looks like it's going to catch."

"You make a fire much better than I do. I've spent hours trying to get the fire at the inn going. I keep telling myself I'll get better at it, but I don't know if that's necessarily true."

"It is. Although, we should talk about the possibility of putting a gas fireplace in at the inn. It would save you a lot of work and trouble."

"I'd hate that; nothing smells as good as a wood fireplace. I just love that scent and the crackling and the coziness. Gas doesn't even begin to come close."

"You're a fire snob," he said as he settled down on the loveseat beside her.

She nodded. "I sure am. I definitely have preferences, and I admire competence in the area whenever I see it."

He knew she was talking about him and couldn't stop a smile from spreading over his face. "I'll keep that in mind. The lady's preferences are important to me."

"As yours are important to me. I really do feel terrible about what I said. I don't usually let my mouth run like that."

"Seriously, it's okay," he said, putting his hand up. It came down on her hand, and somehow their fingers twined together. She'd held his hand before and loved the way it gave her strength and created a warmth that seemed to connect their hearts together. Maybe that was just her fanciful imagination, but it felt that way to her.

"Plus, I don't like the fact that you're blaming yourself. I told you, I was not as patient as I should have been." He sighed. "And when you left the first time, I wish I would have fought harder for you. I wish I would have gone after you, tried to talk to you more, not thought that oh, you'll come around or whatever. I don't even know. I guess I was a little bit hurt that you left to begin with. You're the kind of girl that's worth fighting for."

"Don't blame yourself. I don't know that I would have listened, although I think a girl always does like to be chased a little. It would have been flattering if you would have come after me." She paused, really not sure that would have made a difference, but thinking it probably would have. "It's too late now. Your mistakes, my mistakes. I guess it's nice to think that I'm older now and I won't make any more, but I know that's not true."

"You're allowed to make mistakes. I do appreciate the apology though. Because I wasn't sure if you meant what you said or not."

"I didn't. I admire you for what you've done. I was just lashing out, trying to hurt you, I guess, and I figured that was one way where I could reach you. And I'm sorry. I guess the better you get to know someone, the better you get at finding the spots that hurt them when you are so inclined. I wish I hadn't been inclined."

"It's truly okay. As long as you forgive me for not being patient."

"I'll forgive you on one condition," she said.

He seemed surprised that she would put a condition on it, and his brows lifted as he tilted his head. "Okay?"

"I want you to be done being patient and waiting to kiss me."

He stared at her for a moment. Then his eyes narrowed. "I think you're saying you want me to kiss you now."

"Yes. That's exactly right." She grinned a little and tried to tamp down the nervousness. She hadn't been expecting those exact words to come out of her mouth, although that had been her condition. She felt kind of brave for saying it to begin with and smiled as Lance leaned forward.

"I just want you to know that I love you," Lance said.

"I love you too. Although it's hard for me to believe that you love me when I acted the way I did."

"I think that's what love is, isn't it? To love the good and the bad, and not expect perfection. But when you love someone, you're always striving to be better for them, right?"

She nodded, and their noses bumped.

Then he closed the distance between them and kissed her. Finally, after so many years apart, it felt perfect and right, and also like they were sealing a love that would last a lifetime.

Twenty-Two

The day before the grand opening, Shannon worked in the kitchen with Marina, finalizing what would be on the breakfast buffet and what they would be offering for room service to their paying guests, of which they had a few.

There were two rooms that weren't booked, along with the entire third story, which was not quite finished. Shannon just hadn't had the opportunity to go up and figure out the final touches on the decorations, and several rooms still needed beds and bedding yet.

She'd been working as much as she could, and with a lighter heart now that she and Lance had reconciled. In the evening, once he was done working at the hardware store, he often came over to give her a hand.

She had appreciated it more than she could say.

"I don't know, eggs Benedict are so good, but I don't know if we want anything that complicated. You really can't have them ready in less than fifteen minutes, not if you want the sauce to be fresh," Marina said, biting her lip.

"I think people are willing to wait for—"

She stopped mid-sentence and looked up as a figure entered the kitchen doorway. She hadn't heard the front door of the inn open, although it was unlocked for anyone to come in. They were still getting deliveries, and local people stopped in at any time. In fact, they were expecting Lauren to show up with a last-minute choice for baked goods on the buffet.

"Morison," Shannon said, trying not to have too much antagonism in her voice. But she didn't have a whole lot of time for the man. He'd not left town but had been digging around still.

"Ms. McKay," Morison said. "But you're not really the one I'm interested in. It's her." He pointed at Marina.

Marina gasped, and a hand went to her chest.

Shannon remembered what Marina had said to her about her abusive ex, and she, without thinking, took two steps and inserted her body in front of Marina's. "You have no business here. You can leave."

"It's okay. I'm not doing anything wrong. I just wanted Marina to know that her ex-husband knows that she's alive, and he's offering a substantial reward for her location. He just wants to talk. He wants to make sure she's okay."

Shannon didn't believe that for a second.

"Vincent does not want to talk. Maybe he wants to beat me for being a bad wife, but talking is not his specialty." Marina's words sounded like she was trying to be brave and was almost succeeding.

"Come on. He's not that bad. He's turned over a new leaf. He told me that he realized after you left that he really loves you and doesn't want anything to hurt you. He just wants you back. Because he loves you so much."

"No. I'm not going."

Shannon knew that if Marina decided to go back, she would just be going back to a life of abuse, to a husband who wanted to control her and who probably would be even more enraged now that she'd managed to escape for almost a year.

"You can either come with me on your own, or I will help you," Morison said, emphasizing the word "help."

"No. You heard the lady, she said no. Now you may leave, or I will *help* you." Mateo arrived, appearing behind Morison's shoulder and clamping a hand down on the man.

Shannon held her breath, half expecting Morison to turn around and try to punch Mateo in the face. Maybe she'd watched too many movies. Because Morison froze, and fear flashed across his face.

Apparently, he knew he was out of line to physically threaten Marina.

"What? Are you a sheriff or something?" Morison said, obviously using bravado.

"I think it's pretty much against the law in any state, anywhere, for you to physically touch the woman, especially when she clearly and audibly said no. For you to threaten to do so comes close to a crime. I suggest you leave."

Morison's lips flattened, and he glanced at Marina. "This isn't over."

"Yes, it is. It's over now. We'll be getting a protection from abuse order, and we will be pressing charges if anyone sees you anywhere near this town again. Get in your car, and don't stop until you need gas."

Shannon almost laughed. It sounded so funny, like it came right out of a movie, except it was real, and Marina was obviously terrified. She could feel the woman shaking from behind her.

Mateo was angry. That vein that stood out on his forehead and the tic in his cheek were obvious signs. And Morison was half afraid, half trying to bluff and bravado his way through.

She swallowed hard. She'd never been in a scene like this. Her ex had been terrible, but he hadn't been abusive, thankfully. She couldn't imagine what Marina had gone through. Especially if the man was so desperate that he would hire someone and send him out to try to drag her back. What was it about her saying no that the man didn't understand?

Morison glanced at Mateo and then made a show of getting his shoulder out from underneath Mateo's hand and then walking around the man and out the door.

The front door of the inn had barely closed when Mateo rushed over to Marina, completely ignoring Shannon.

"Are you okay? I saw him go through town, and when he made the turn to the inn, I got here as fast as I could."

"Thank you so much. I do think he was getting ready to drag me with him, whether I wanted to go or not and even though Shannon was here as a witness."

"I think you're right. I highly recommend you not be by yourself, until we're sure that he understood my threats were sincere. And I think we need to go to the police. You can get a restraining order, and you can file charges. That should be enough to keep him away from you."

Marina pulled both lips in. "He always said it would be worse for me if I ever went to the authorities. And considering how bad it was to begin with..."

"I'll be there. I won't let him hurt you. This is the only way to keep him away from you."

"He just left." Homer's voice came from the doorway. "I passed him on my way here."

"Good."

"I couldn't help but overhear what you were saying, and I agree. We need to file charges; we need to get this on the record. And the only way Marina has of defeating him is getting the authorities involved. I also agree that she shouldn't be alone."

"Yeah," Mateo said, looking hard at Marina.

"I also looked up both men. Morison is shady. He's got a rap sheet of his own. Vincent looks pretty good on paper, but I did manage to dig up a few things, hints that he might have a pretty explosive temper. Charges that have been dropped, and one interesting-looking payoff-type thing. I might be able to get more if I need to dig deeper."

"That sounds like enough," Mateo said.

"I'm pretty sure I passed him on the way out," Pastor Garnett said as he stepped in the door with Josiah beside him.

"Yeah. I'm pretty sure he's gone," Mateo said.

Voices broke out as everyone gave their opinion on what Marina should do, and Shannon waited while Marina seemed to waver back and forth. It was obvious she was afraid of what her ex might do, of making him mad, and of the pain he could inflict on her, but it was also obvious that she knew that everyone was right.

Finally, Mateo and Homer left with Marina between them to go file a report at the police station. They told Shannon that they would let her know if they needed her to show up, or perhaps an officer would be dispatched to come take a statement from her, since she was a witness to the entire event.

She offered to go, but Marina knew how busy they were and how much they needed to do to get ready for the next day, and she insisted that Shannon stay.

By the end of the day, the entire town had rallied around Marina once they had understood that she was hiding from domestic abuse. Everyone was glad that Marina had decided to stand and fight, and pledged to stand behind her. Mateo was by her side the entire time she was giving her statement and doing the police report, and he offered to stay at the inn, guarding it all night while catching catnaps at his gym during the day.

Shannon didn't think that was necessary, since they did have a security system installed, and it engaged every night at midnight. The townspeople decided that someone would be around until midnight every night until they got the thing worked out.

Shannon was glad to see Marina facing her fear, and she felt like she and Marina had matured at the same time. She had faced hers when she had gone to apologize to Lance and when she'd asked him to kiss her.

She wasn't sure that she was totally cured from the idea of allowing fear to control her life, but every victory gave her strength for another, even harder one. That much was true, and she shared that with Marina that night before they went to bed.

"Tomorrow's the opening, and I think we're ready," Marina finally said once they had talked about her ex and the different scenarios that could happen.

"I think we are too. I wish I had more rooms ready. I think we might have been able to be sold out, and that would have been a really exciting opening day."

"But you've got more done than I ever thought you would. When I first walked in, I didn't know how in the world you would be able to open the inn before next year at the earliest."

"I know. The town really rallied around us." She looked around at the beautifully decorated room, with gourds and pumpkins and fall colors lighting everything up, glowing gently in the soft night lights of the inn. It was absolutely amazing, and she couldn't have done it without the town behind her, but especially Lance. She hadn't talked to him a whole lot that day, although he seemed to hover close in the evening, like he was afraid for her. Or just wanted to be there for her.

Maybe once the inn opened and things settled down, they would have more time to discuss what they were going to do in their future. She hoped that marriage would be a part of that. But he hadn't said anything. And they were kind of old. Too old to start a family. Too old to have those young-person hopes and dreams of spending a lifetime together. They could just spend what was left of their lifetime.

She hated to be depressed about that and tried to look at it in a positive way. This was the first day of the rest of her life, and she wanted every day to be spent with Lance. She needed to tell him that.

Twenty-Three

"I think I have everything ready. We've got food on the buffet, the rooms have all been checked and double-checked, Marina is making something amazing, Lauren brought snacks and baked goods, Vera has been arranging flowers, Skyler is helping with the table settings, and I feel like I'm forgetting something, but I can't think of what it is." Shannon tried to tamp down her anxiety as she looked up into Lance's face.

He smiled and put a hand on either side of her shoulders. "You are going to be amazing. Everything is ready. And if it's not, we'll handle it on the fly. This is going to be the best opening any inn has ever seen, and it's because so much hard work has gone into it, but also love and companionship and camaraderie like only Raspberry Ridge can do."

His words were comforting and calm, and they soothed her nerves immediately.

She stepped closer and put her arms around his neck, drawing him down to her and touching her lips with his. "You're the best thing that ever happened to me. Thank you."

They pulled apart, just enough to be able to look into each other's eyes and smile.

Then they broke apart but held hands as they walked through the inn one last time. The kitchen was buzzing with activity, with Marina in charge of it all. There was some flour on the counter, something a little sticky on the floor, and Marina had what looked like chocolate on her forehead, but she looked calm and cool and collected, and Mateo was at her side, making sure that anything she needed or wanted was within her reach immediately.

"They look good together, don't they?" Shannon said as they left the kitchen.

"Marina and Mateo?" Lance asked, as though he hadn't really noticed.

"Yeah. Mateo told me that he was going to ask Marina to officially be his girlfriend today. I kind of thought that perhaps another day might work out better, since this one was going to be pretty chaotic, but I didn't want to discourage him, because I know Marina really is hoping he will."

"I say don't put it off. You never know what might happen," Lance said.

Shannon felt a little bit bad about that, because he had admitted that he wished he would have gone after her all those years ago. Followed her to college somehow, instead of staying home and keeping his word to his mom and taking care of his sister.

But everything worked out for the best. She was sure of it. Just sometimes a person did end up with a few regrets. But it was best to focus on the positive things in a person's life. Because there was always so much to be thankful for.

They finished walking through the inn, admiring the beautiful fall decorations, the cozy fire in the fireplace despite the dreary day outside. It was November, and a cold rain was falling. It could have been snow if the temperature had been just ten degrees cooler, which Shannon wouldn't have minded.

Still, the fall decorations, the cozy atmosphere, the camaraderie of so many people made her heart burst with happiness.

"Shannon! Shannon!" Claire hurried up to her.

"What?" Shannon asked, looking around to see what she might have forgotten. She knew she had forgotten something.

"I just got word from Chicago that a big paper, plus an online restaurant site, and another online hotel site are all sending reviewers out to be given a tour of your inn and to write up reviews in their various publications. I wanted to give you a heads-up, although I know you've already done everything that you possibly could to make this day a success. I just didn't want you to be blindsided when they showed up." She glanced out the front door. "Looks like they're here."

"Oh my goodness, Lance, what am I gonna do?"

"You don't have to do anything. Everything's already been taken care of. You're gonna be just fine."

Shannon wasn't entirely sure that was true, but she took a deep breath and drew strength from the man beside her. He was such a rock.

"How does my hair look?" she asked, realizing she hadn't checked it since about four AM that morning.

"Gorgeous. Absolutely stunning," Lance said.

"I think you wouldn't tell me the truth," she said, laughing. His answer made her happy though, just because it made her think that no matter how she looked, she looked good to him.

"Your hair looks fine. I know Shelley Bogart personally, and I'll greet her, and then I'll introduce you guys, okay?" Claire said as she made to walk toward the front door.

Shannon nodded. "I appreciate it."

She looked over at Lance. "Please don't leave me."

"I'm right here. This is my spot all day long, unless you send me somewhere."

She couldn't imagine anything that would inspire her to send him from her side. And she definitely appreciated his presence as Claire introduced her to Shelley and the other two reviewers. She took them on a short tour and then invited them to check out the inn themselves. She said that their guests could be arriving anytime after three, and a quick glance at her phone indicated that they only had thirty minutes.

The reviewers tasted some of the food, talked to some of the townspeople, and wandered around the spacious inn, looking at the various decorations and the decor in all of the rooms. Shannon explained that the third story wasn't quite ready, but they were welcome to go up there if they wanted to.

The reviewers seemed impressed that such a small town had such a beautiful inn, and Shannon took great delight in telling them how the townspeople had come together, helping her after she had made an impulse buy with her divorce settlement.

She didn't want to bring her ex into it, and she carefully didn't mention his name, but she figured they could probably dig it up if they wanted to.

She thought about asking them to leave him completely out of it, but it was what it was.

One of the reviewers left, but the other two sat in chairs, and Shannon lost track of them as the first guests arrived.

She was standing behind the front desk to greet them as they checked into their room, and she gave them key cards and explained about the availability of baked goods all day long on the buffet, as well as the time of breakfast in the morning. She also told them that there was a list of things that they could order for room service in their room and pointed out the services the town of Raspberry Ridge offered, including the horse-drawn rides, delicious baked goods, and handcrafted woodcrafts.

She was excited to be able to promote the folks in the town, after the way they had supported her through everything.

The couple was sweet and kind and seemed genuinely interested in what the town offered. The man confided that they were thinking about moving away from the big city to start a family and had been looking at property up in Blackberry Bay, which was just a short drive away.

"It seems to be less congested than Blueberry Beach or even Strawberry Sands. And the fact that there is so much to do right here makes me think that we really wouldn't be getting away from anything other than the big-city annoyances."

"Blackberry Bay is very beautiful, and you're right, there's plenty to do all around but not so much activity that it feels that it has lost its small-town feel. It's very much like Raspberry Ridge."

The couple wandered off. The next three couples arrived one after the other, and she was busy for the next hour, answering questions and showing people around.

By the time five o'clock had rolled around, she realized that the town was implementing an impromptu buffet around the large table in the meeting room, with Marina having made her famous Nutella banana bread, along with several pans of lasagna, which were complemented by various dishes the townspeople had brought. It was like a church social, only inside.

Twenty-Four

"Hey there, have a minute?" Lance stuck his head in the kitchen door where Marina and Shannon were talking about the menu for the next weekend. The guests had left on Monday morning, and they'd cleaned everything. While they had two guests staying in rooms currently, she anticipated that the weekdays would be less busy than the weekends.

"I sure do," she said, giving Marina a glance with lifted brows. Marina smiled and nodded. There was a glow about her that a woman in love often had. She hadn't heard anything else from her ex or from Morison, and the police report had been filed. Hopefully that was all it was going to take to keep her ex from bothering her again.

"You might wanna put on a coat, we need to go outside."

"Okay," she said, mystified as to what would cause him to need to go out.

It was a nice, beautiful, sunny day, but the temperatures were definitely cool enough that one would want to wear a coat for any extended activity outside.

"Can I ask where we're going?"

"You can," Lance said with a wink.

She laughed and then rolled her eyes.

Her hand slipped into his as he opened the door for her, and she stepped out into the beautiful fall day.

Thanksgiving was the next week, and both of her children were coming in for it.

She hadn't spoken to her ex and hadn't asked either one of them if he was doing anything. She really didn't care. He had his own life now with his new girlfriend, and she heard that the girlfriend was expecting a baby.

She wouldn't want to be starting over with a new family at her age. Not like she even could. But she supposed with James's twenty-five-year-old girlfriend, that was probably something James was going to be dealing with—children who were decades apart.

Maybe she'd get a chance to talk to her children about how they felt about that, but there really wasn't anything she could do.

"It's a beautiful day, isn't it?" Lance said as they started out.

"It sure is. And I'm glad that the hustle and bustle of opening day is over, but... I can't believe the reservations that are pouring in. We had a whole rash of them this morning."

"It might be because of this," he said, holding up his phone and scrolling until he found what he wanted, then started to read, "'The grand opening of the Sunset Inn was a spectacular extravaganza, showcasing the close-knit community of the town of Raspberry Ridge, along with the brilliant culinary mastery of Marina Castellano, renowned chef from the Corella family, hailing from upstate New York. This little gem along the gorgeous, majestic shores of Lake Michigan is the perfect weekend getaway for any couple interested in romance, as well as the slower pace of a rural community, while still having plenty to do.'"

The review went on, talking about the amazing decor in each room, the beautiful views, amazing food, and the quaint town, but the atmosphere was something that the reviewer touched on more than once.

"It sounds to me like I have the whole town of Raspberry Ridge to thank for the total success of opening day."

"Yes. That was one of the reviewers. The other two had glowing reviews as well. They all posted this morning. I wasn't sure whether you knew or not."

"I hadn't even thought to look. I guess for some reason I was thinking it would be weeks before they got the reviews in and up."

"It's the age of the internet. Things happen a lot faster now," Lance said with a knowing look.

"I suppose they do. Wow. I don't even know what to say. That's truly a testament to the spirit of Raspberry Ridge."

"And you. Because you had a vision to begin with."

"I don't know if you could say that, considering that it was a spur-of-the-moment decision at two o'clock in the morning from a woman who was rather depressed about her divorce and unsure about her future as her children were all making their lives away from her, and she felt abandoned and alone and over the hill."

"That doesn't describe the woman I'm looking at," Lance said as he slowed their pace, and she realized that they were standing on top of the bluffs where they'd spent so much time in their youth.

"I love this place," she said, lifting her face to the breeze and closing her eyes as the sun shone down on her, and the clean, fresh air filled her lungs.

"And you're beautiful. I love you," Lance said.

She opened her eyes, smiling up at him and expecting him to kiss her, but instead, he dropped to one knee.

Her eyes widened as she realized what he was doing. A hand went to her throat.

Was she ready for this? She hadn't really thought about it, other than... Yes, she'd longed to have a marriage and a life with this man.

She knew what she was going to say before he even pulled the little box out and opened it to show a glittering ring.

It wasn't anything too fancy, but it was perfect for her, and she was amazed at what a perfect ring he had picked out for her.

"It's been a long time. I've loved you forever. Will you spend the rest of your life with me?" he asked, his words being swept away by the wind but carried to her on the wings of love.

"Yes. Absolutely yes. I couldn't think of anything I'd like to do more," she said as he straightened, and that's when he kissed her.

They stood there for a while, lost in their embrace, before he pulled back and said, "I'd really like to have a wedding that's not too far in the future."

"Before winter?" she asked, grinning when his brows lifted like he hadn't been expecting her to want it that fast.

"I don't want you to rush it. You should have everything you want."

"I had everything the first time. All the bells and the whistles and the dress and the cake and everything. And it didn't make our marriage last any longer than if we had just stood in front of the preacher with nothing. I'd rather... I'd rather just have the town here and be married in the church. Maybe a Christmas wedding. Christmas decorations would be beautiful."

"Then you should have it," Lance said. "And Christmas is perfect. I think I can wait six weeks."

"All right then. Six weeks—you and me, meet at the church."

They laughed together. And she could hardly believe that this man that she'd loved so many years ago was finally going to marry her.

The news of their engagement spread like wildfire, especially the weekend when Pastor Garrett announced it from the pulpit during the Sunday service.

The reaction from the community was everything Shannon would have expected. The congregation broke out into spontaneous applause as Pastor Garrett announced it, and after church, she was inundated with offers of help. She accepted them all. Lauren wanted to bake the cake, Marina insisted she get to cater the wedding, and Grace actually offered to make a wedding dress.

"Better than that, I wanted to wear my mom's wedding dress for my first wedding, but my mother-in-law said it wasn't fancy enough, so it's remained boxed and in storage all these years. I'd like to get it out and do whatever altering it needs in order to fit." She certainly wasn't the slender, whipcord-thin girl she had been when she'd been married the first time. "It might be a little bit complicated, because I'm not the size I was back then, and I'm sure my mother was thin as well."

She definitely had the middle-age spread going, but she didn't need to admit that out loud today.

"Whatever it needs, I can figure it out," Grace said with confidence.

"It seems like everybody's going to have a hand in this wedding," Lance said as Becky and Rodney came up, offering a carriage ride to the bride and groom from the church to the inn where they assumed the reception was going to be held.

"So fancy," Shannon said as they walked away, feeling like her whole face was glowing. Along with her heart.

"You would do the same for everyone else, and don't think for one second that that isn't benefiting everyone. I heard Josiah saying that his business has been thriving, as well as Claire's husband's. Apparently the guests have taken our suggestions to heart and have given their business to people in town. I actually heard that Dominic might be building a house for the first couple who booked at your inn, up in Blackberry Bay. It's not a small thing," Lance said with his brows raised.

"You're going to be my sister," Katie said, putting her arm through Shannon's and smiling hugely.

"I am, and I can't wait," Shannon said, pulling Katie close into a hug. Katie had been such an encourager when Shannon had needed to apologize to Lance. She probably would have done it without Katie's encouragement, but Katie broke the ice and made it easy.

"We don't want to do a double wedding, but I did want to let you know that Mateo asked me last night to marry him, and I said yes," Marina said as she leaned down and spoke softly in Shannon's ear. "We're going to keep it to ourselves until next week and let you have today all to yourself. But I just wanted you to know, because I'm overwhelmed with excitement. I was married to a terrible person for such a long time that I really don't know how to act around a man who respects me and gives me the love and kindness that I deserve."

Shannon smiled at Marina's happiness and pulled her into a huge hug. "Congratulations. You couldn't have found a better man."

And she meant that. Mateo was awesome, and he was absolutely perfect for Marina. "I know he's going to treat you the way you should be treated."

They pulled back, looking into each other's eyes, and Shannon felt blessed to have such a good friend, who worked alongside her.

"We're going to have to talk about your salary, too," she said.

Knowing that with all of the guests who were pouring into the inn, she was going to be able to afford it.

"We can if you want to. But I'm not worried about it. I have a lawyer, and he felt like I would be getting a pretty big settlement from my divorce from Vincent. That's if Vincent doesn't want me to go public with all of the accusations that I have, which I'm sure he won't." Marina looked smug, and Shannon shook her head with a smile on her face. After everything that Marina had suffered, she hoped she got millions from the settlement.

She deserved it.

"I think I'd like to have you alone for a little while, if you think you might be able to spare some time for me this afternoon," Lance said as he slipped an arm around her, and they walked out of the church together.

"You have my entire day. It's at your disposal," Shannon said, leaning into him. She couldn't think of anything she'd rather do than spend the rest of her life with this man, and if it started today, that was just fine with her.

Twenty-Five

"Oh, Mom, you look beautiful," Emma said as she stood from arranging the train on Shannon's wedding gown. "I love you," she said, hugging her gently, careful not to mess up Shannon's dress. Shannon didn't care, she hugged her daughter tightly, so happy that Emma had agreed to be her maid of honor.

"I love you too. And this day wouldn't be complete without you. Thank you for making time to come."

"Mother, of course. And I have some good news I want to tell you later."

"Good news? Tell me now," Shannon said as she heard the music begin.

"I can't really say, but it has to do with people you love coming to Blackberry Bay."

"Mom, are you ready?" Alex said, looking so tall and handsome in his suit as he held his elbow out for her to take it.

Her dad wasn't alive to walk her down the aisle, but Alex had graciously agreed to. His wife, who was expecting, sat in the second row, looking down the church aisle expectantly, waiting for them to come.

"You're gorgeous," Marina said. She was the last of the ladies who had been helping Shannon get dressed. Grace, Claire, Vera, and so many others had been in the room with her, encouraging her and just spending the last few minutes before it was time to start.

They were all sitting with their spouses now, and Lance stood at the end of the aisle, looking back, love shining in his eyes.

"I'm ready," Shannon said, glancing one more time at Lance, before she looked at her son and smiled.

Emma had already started to walk, and everyone stood as Alex and Shannon stepped out of the vestibule.

The strains of the music flowed over the church as Shannon walked by so many familiar and beloved faces. The Christmas decorations were perfect, and it was a beautiful, absolutely amazing December evening with light snow falling.

Everything was ready for the reception at the inn, and the guests who had arrived to spend their Christmas Eve at the inn were invited as well.

Vera and Dominic had offered to set up something in the healing garden, heaters and a tent, but as nice as that would have been, the church felt like the right spot.

Pastor Garrett stood at the end of the aisle as Alex handed her off to Lance, and he told them to clasp hands.

As they stood looking at each other, repeating the vows that were as old and timeless as weddings themselves, she couldn't help but glow and think that this time, it truly would be until death did them part. After all, Lance had been in love with her forever, and he'd never wavered. She had been lured away, but she knew she would never be again. She understood exactly what she had in Lance and that men like him were few and far between. And she was blessed to have him.

Soon they were pronounced man and wife, and they shared a chaste kiss as the audience cheered before the photographer took some pictures, and then they stepped out into the carriage that awaited, pulled by elegant and beautiful horses, snuggled under warm, cozy robes. The falling snow made the scene picturesque as they held hands and laughed together on their way to the inn.

It was a short ride, less than ten minutes, but Shannon felt like a princess as Rodney opened the little door of the carriage and helped her out.

She and Lance walked up to the inn, which they now owned together, and into the feast that awaited them. Marina's catering was exceptional, the dining room perfectly decorated and amazing for dancing as they finished eating and slid the tables to the side, and the celebration felt like a fairy tale. A perfect ending to Shannon's long and somewhat winding road, and while she knew that the rest of her life was not going to be completely smooth sailing, there was the idea that perhaps Emma was moving back to Blackberry Bay, or maybe she meant Alex was. Shannon wasn't sure, but regardless, the idea that people she loved would be close by couldn't have made the evening better.

They stayed until everyone left, and it was after midnight. But neither one of them wanted the day to end, and they ended up standing on the porch of the inn, wrapped in one of the cozy blankets, watching the snow fall, and talking about their hopes and their dreams, the moonlight glistening off the lake in the distance as they discussed their future together. It was the wedding of her dreams, with the man of her dreams, and Shannon couldn't have been happier to have come through the dark night and into the most beautiful time of her life.

"Coming home to Raspberry Ridge was the best decision I ever made." She looked up at Lance, smiling into his eyes.

"I have to agree with that. It's the best decision that you made for me too."

He leaned down and kissed her forehead, and a glow of warmth and contentment grew within Shannon. While she knew that life would not be perfect, she was grateful, from the very bottom of her soul, for everything the Lord had done but especially for her husband and that they had been given a second chance at life and love.

Thanks so much for spending time with me in Raspberry Ridge! I've loved sharing the lakeside breezes and sweet love stories with you!

If you'd enjoy more second chance romance, summer sun and tight knit community, please check out Seaside Sisterhood HERE!

A Gift from Jessie

View this code through your smart phone camera to be taken to a page where you can download a FREE ebook when you sign up to get updates from Jessie Gussman! Find out why people say, "Jessie's is the only newsletter I open and read" and "You make my day brighter. Love, love, love reading your newsletters. I don't know where you find time to write books. You are so busy living life. A true blessing." and "I know from now on that I can't be drinking my morning coffee while reading your newsletter – I laughed so hard I sprayed it out all over the table!"

Claim your free book from Jessie!

Escape to more faith-filled romance series by Jessie Gussman!

The Complete Sweet Water, North Dakota Reading Order:

Series One: Sweet Water Ranch Western Cowboy Romance (11 book series)

Series Two: Coming Home to North Dakota (12 book series)

Series Three: Flyboys of Sweet Briar Ranch in North Dakota (13 book series)

Series Four: Sweet View Ranch Western Cowboy Romance (10 book series)

Spinoffs and More! Additional Series You'll Love:

Jessie's First Series: Sweet Haven Farm (4 book series)

Small-Town Romance: The Baxter Boys (5 book series)

Bad-Boy Sweet Romance: Richmond Rebels Sweet Romance (3 book series)

Sweet Water Spinoff: Cowboy Crossing (9 book series)

Small Town Romantic Comedy: Good Grief, Idaho (5 book series)

True Stories from Jessie's Farm: Stories from Jessie Gussman's Newsletter (3 book series)

Reader-Favorite! Sweet Beach Romance: Blueberry Beach (8 book series)

Blueberry Beach Spinoff: Strawberry Sands (10 book series)

From Strawberry Sands to: Raspberry Ridge (12 book series)

Swoonfully Jolly Holiday Stories:

Holiday Romance: Cowboy Mountain Christmas (6 book series)

Cowboy Mountain Christmas Spinoff: A Heartland Cowboy Christmas (9 book series)

New and Much Loved: Mistletoe Meadows (4 books and counting!)

Laughing Through the Snow: Christmas Tree, PA Sweet Romcoms (6 short reads)